A CERTAIN KIND OF LUCK

A Certain Kind

of Luck

STORIES

B.R. Lewis

Paperback ISBN: 9781965412466

Cover art and design by Jacob Arms

Published by Broken Tribe Press
William K. Lawrence, Editor in Chief
Lawrence Landing Company
Raleigh, North Carolina 27609
United States of America
www.brokentribepress.com

Broken Tribe Press is a proud member of

Independent Book Publishers Association
 and
Community of Literary Magazines and Presses

For my family

CONTENTS

Narrow River

Leland turned the key in the ignition. The old green pickup sputtered, clearing its throat as it rumbled to life. Once the engine would run without his foot on the gas pedal, he stepped out of the truck's cab, crunching the brittle, frosted dirt beneath his boots. The sky was clear, a hopeful sign that the early chill would burn off with the rising sun. He scraped his windshield as the truck warmed up, then cleared the side windows and mirrors.

Before he climbed back into the truck, Leland cracked the canopy's rear window. Inside he saw the lumber and tools, precisely where he had left them after visiting True Value during lunch on Friday. Only the long beams had been moved. He had cut those into the required lengths the night before, trying to keep this project from lasting all weekend.

Back in the cab, Leland warmed his hands over the dashboard heater and sipped directly from his thermos of coffee. The fan belt squealed as he put the truck in gear and headed east on Highway 14, toward the county line.

Arnold had called him at the garage on Tuesday, in a near religious fervor about violations of tribal rights and the Treaty of 1855. His cousin was furious because the platform below Husum Falls was gone. The lumber had already washed down the White Salmon, on its way to the Columbia. *I hope it jams the lock*, Arnold barked through the receiver, *or sinks some goddamn Mayflower's wind board.* Leland sighed, twisting the phone cord between his fingers. He'd built the platform a month ago and it had yet to be used.

He didn't ask if there was any evidence that the stand had been torn down. Arnold's slurred speech, peppered with curses, made his suspicions clear. The river was high, but the spring flows weren't wild enough to wash out the platform. And Leland didn't need his cousin to point out the obvious suspect. *Everybody knows Josh Sanders pulled it down.* The owner of White Water Adventures had organized the coalition of rafting companies. He had vowed to reverse the decision to allow the platforms by any means.

Leland told his cousin not to worry, that he would repair the structure as soon as he could. He couldn't make it out to the falls until Saturday. The garage was backed up with work and he couldn't afford to close it up during the week. Husum was forty minutes from the garage, and building the walkway wasn't an after-dinner project. Not that the delay made any difference, since there were no fish anyway.

During the course of the week, several other cousins called, along with his grandfather, Norman. They called the garage so often that Leland started to wonder if he would ever get any work done. He was already tense. Susan had been on him all week, convinced he was dragging out repairs so he could overcharge for her Volvo's front end work. The sales rep was always impatient; that's why she took a corner too tight and clipped a short retaining wall. Actually, he wasn't charging enough. She glared and tapped her high heels each time he asked her to wait while he answered the phone.

The calls continued when he was home, eating his frozen dinners in front of the TV. His grandfather was particularly livid. He was going to drive the 120 miles from his HUD home in Wapato and rebuild the platform himself. All he needed was someone to load up the camper. *Just let me stay out there a few nights with my shotgun, Lee, and we'll see if anyone has the balls to tear it down.* Leland barely managed to talk him down, reassuring him that he had everything under control.

Highway 14 snaked along the northern walls of the Columbia River Gorge, occasionally dipping down to the river. On the shotgun seat of the cab sat a red truck stop baseball cap, embroidered with the image of a peace pipe and *Native Pride* in block letters across the bill. Norman had given it to him. The old man had jumped at the chance to volunteer his grandson to build the traditional fishing platform on the White Salmon River. Norman was a member of the tribal fishing council, and claimed that their family had always fished this stretch of water, before the Condit Dam. When Leland initially tried to decline the honor, the 84-year-old said he would build it himself, rather than tell the council his own kin refused.

Leland relented, choosing not to call his bluff. Norman immediately brightened, produced the hat, and shoved it down on Leland's short hair. That was the only time he had worn it. Beyond the cap, there would be no compensation, other than the gratitude of the tribe. He saw little honor in the task, or even why it was necessary to build a platform on a river that hadn't seen a single salmon for more than 100 years. With no fish ladder, the dam had blocked the salmon from the river and they had wisely gone elsewhere to spawn. But he was the only son of Norman's oldest son, and God only knew where his father was these days. So the responsibility fell to him.

Leland crossed into Klickitat County and turned left onto the Highway 141 spur. The wide gray expanse of the Columbia in the predawn light vanished from the rearview mirror after the first bend. The two-lane road wound its way toward the town of Husum. A rusted sign pointed to the Northwestern Lake boat ramp; someone had forgotten that the lake was gone, drained away when the dam was breached. Near the Falls Bridge, cafes, bed and breakfasts and the storefronts of commercial rafting companies lined one side of the street. A nowhere place, he thought, where people lived to be disconnected.

The White Salmon cut down through the foothills of Pahto (Mount Adams), in the borderland between the eastern and western sides of the state. Husum Falls was a transitional place, where pine and fir trees mingled. He had camped in these woods one fall, stalking elk and eating government surplus cheese sandwiches with Norman. His father was already gone by then, and he looked so much like Norman's son that Leland's mother decided she couldn't stand to look at him anymore. Without hesitation his grandfather had taken him.

Over the years, Norman had taken him camping and hunting, trying to teach him self-reliance, stressing the importance of remembering where he came from. During one of those trips, in the woods near Husum, Leland and Norman had brought down a five point bull elk. As they set about skinning and preparing the meat, the game warden pulled up. He wanted to see their tags. They didn't have any; Norman saw no reason to buy a license for a right he was already guaranteed. *All the usual and accustomed places,* his grandfather had intoned, looking the officer in the eye. But the warden persisted, *This ain't the rez.* The meat was impounded for the warden's freezer. They loaded up the camper and went home early, his grandfather cussing all the way back to Wapato about how the cowboys always win.

Leland parked at the gravel turnaround near the bridge and heard the dull roar of the falls. A gravel path led to stone stairs to the right bank of the river. The trail was not meant for him. It was built for conservative kayakers who wished to launch below the falls, bank fishermen, and hot-blooded teenagers in need of a make out spot. The county would not have constructed a trail to allow easy reclamation of native rights along the narrow river. Nevertheless, he appreciated not having to traverse a steep slope of crumbling dirt and loose rock to reach the rocky edge. Leland unloaded his planks, tools and a small cooler.

The sun was barely beginning to peek over the hills. Whoever dismantled the platform had been thorough; not a single support beam remained in place. The drop frothed with white water and filled the air with a fine mist as the river spilled over clean granite and basalt, unimpeded by his handiwork. Husum Falls was divided into three chutes by a pair of rounded boulders that protruded from the river like worn canine teeth. The platform had to span fifteen feet, from the shore to the outside corner of the center chute, over where the water pooled below the falls.

A cool northeastern breeze funneled down the riverbed and sent a shiver through Leland's body as he began to construct the scaffolding. He buried the ends of two sturdy beams on either side of a broad flat stone near the water. Ashes from the fireplace hearth and dirt from his ancestral home---the flowerbed near Norman's front steps---were mixed with the soil that covered the ends, as his grandfather instructed. Fortunately, he still had some of the potting soil from the last time he'd buried the beams. Next, stilt legs were fitted precisely into natural notches in the stones. A series of angled crossbeams between these legs would reinforce the structure's frame. The platform would be held to the shore by the tension of its parts.

By midmorning the canyon warmed under the early spring sun. Leland removed his jacket. He wiped the sweat from his brow and stretched his stiff lower back. His work had gone largely undisturbed; only a few cars passed, and a handful of joggers rattled the bridge deck over his left shoulder. He knelt on the uneven surface of the rock and began to nail the planks to the frame. The sound of his hammer echoed off the foothills, creating a steady rhythm in the still morning air.

These platforms were common on the Columbia, under the Bridge of the Gods in Stevenson, where he lived and worked. In his youth, Norman told him how Coyote had taught his people to harvest the salmon. Starving, cunning Coyote exploited the sex drive of the fish, as the Coho and Chinook blindly marched up the river to spawn. The trickster created waterfalls and forced the salmon to the surface. Then he constructed the first platform out of poplar and willow branches and slung a net below its frame. Coyote built a fire in the shade of a great pine tree and waited for the net to fill with his slippery prey. And he taught these methods to the Yakama.

The story always reminded Leland of the Husum Falls hunting trip, Norman sitting near the campfire. The fire reflected in his thick glasses, and he had a somber look on his face as he watched the flames dance. *These are our lands Lee*, he said, using his medicine man's voice; *they are a part of you.*

Leland had never fished with a net. Nor did he think it was likely he ever would. His grandfather had described the process of hoisting the heavy, fish-filled seines as backbreaking. Between the slight shifting of the platform and the slickness of the planks, a man was just as likely to drown as to catch enough fish for his whole family. The last time Leland had fished, he had been a child standing on the shores of the Yakima River with Norman. A single rod and reel between them. They caught nothing and picked up some burgers on the way home.

Even if you managed to catch a net full of salmon, what the hell would you do with all those fish? Leland pictured his lazy Klickitat cousins, hung over, sitting on their fat asses in lawn chairs surrounded by coolers. He couldn't imagine them pulling a loaded net out of the water. They peddled salmon to whites at the in-lieu site above Bonneville Dam, or in the Charcoal Burger parking lot. Their jeans were stained with guts, and their shirts permanently reeked of fish oil. Chief Char-O-kee, the restaurant's cartoon Indian mascot, smiled over them with his twin braids, red headband with a single feather at the back, potbelly protruding above his loincloth.

On command, a fish hawker would play noble shaman for the tourists, especially if he also sold dream catchers and other trinkets. Hands stretched toward heaven, he would tell garbled tales of the gods, especially Tyhee Saghalie, and his two sons, Pahto and Wy'east. All people were united by a land bridge across the river, before the jealous sons forced their father to destroy the connection. To Leland, the fish peddlers possessed a self-righteous air, as if impressing whites with folklore somehow preserved their cultural heritage. He would rather break his back in the garage than listen to any white call him chief or Tonto, or try to barter for fresh salmon with whiskey.

By noon the platform protruded five feet over the water. Leland felt the morning's work in his knees. Over his left shoulder, the low murmur of congregating voices floated to him from the steel bridge. Husum Falls was the highlight of White Salmon rafting trips. Leland knew that most tour companies stopped just above the falls, to let off those who were too young or too timid to take the plunge. These groups walked to the bridge downstream of the falls to watch the others drop. One such group, probably one of the first of the season, gathered around a perky guide. Leland stopped hammering and listened to her bubbly voice:

"The White Salmon River was named for the pale color of salmon carcasses after the fish have spawned. It's estimated that nearly 25,000 people raft Husum Falls each year, making it the largest commercially run falls in the United States. Oh, on your right you can see a member of the Yakeema Tribe constructing a traditional fishing platform. Since the removal of the Condit Dam three years ago, eight miles downstream, the tribe remains hopeful that the namesake fish of the river will return."

The group broke into individual conversations that blended with the steady babbling of the river. Some wondered aloud why Leland didn't wear his hair long. Others admired the falls but complained of the chill. A few tried to get Leland to wave, as if he were part of the tour. The platform creaked and shifted slightly beneath him as he crawled forward, assembling the structure section by section. He needed to place another set of legs in the water, to brace the overhang where the netman would stand.

As he stood to retrieve a post from the shore, Leland noticed the crowd's silence. He turned and saw the red raft poised, ready to plummet down the center chute. The raft wobbled, unbalanced by an odd number of passengers, as it made its descent. From the top of the chute it slid over the smooth rock tongue of Husum Falls, then dropped the first three feet. The guides shouted commands to the amateur rafters dressed in bright yellow life vests and gray helmets. Frantically, the oars on the right stabbed the choppy waters, in a desperate attempt to shove off concealed boulders and maneuver toward the left bank. The raft took the last drop and landed against the pool with a loud slap, audible even over the constant noise of the water.

Leland visualized the placement of the constructed platform. The vessel would have clipped the outside corner. He wondered if that contact would have been enough to flip the raft as it spun around under the influence of the unbalanced load. The helmets and life jackets all bore the insignia of the outfitter, White Water Adventures. The white circular logo included the name written in slanted letters encompassed by a cresting wave. The raft's master looked back at the unfinished platform; Leland could tell he was also imagining the completed structure. On the bridge the crowd cheered and waved before being led toward the rendezvous point down stream.

How many careless boaters would be flipped by his platform? How many rubber rafts ruined? Once the brace legs were set, the near chute, popular with kayakers, would be completely blocked. Leland knew this deck wasn't the only obstruction he had been charged to build. Eventually, smaller platforms would hug the shore, allowing better access for hand nets near the outer edges of the pool. The final stage was a short platform, to the shallow rapids above the drop.

Leland hadn't attended the hearings about the multiple-use plan for Husum Falls. He knew their tension and bitterness second hand, from phone calls with relatives back on the reservation, conversations with customers, or newspaper stories. The Yakama delegation had refuted pie charts and economic bottom lines by invoking the ghosts of Celilo and ancient treaties. Finally, after months of debate, the Department of Fish and Wildlife reluctantly admitted that the tribe had priority. Even when white governments declared they had no reason to interfere, Norman scoffed, reminding his grandson that had never stopped them before. Since Leland didn't fish, he had only a passing interest in the issue.

Then Norman showed up in Stevenson, to personally deliver the good news: Their family would resume its traditional role as the keepers of the White Salmon platforms. They sat in Leland's living room, his grandfather grinning, with a cooler between his legs and an eagle feather in his wide brimmed hat. Gray braids hung down on either side of his weathered face. The cooler held a jar of salmon eggs, two dead jack salmon, dirt from the flowerbed, and braided sage grass.

As he leveled the next section of frame, Leland remembered again how he tried to talk his way out of the job. The platform wasn't important to the family. This river, the salmon, if they ever returned, mattered little to their people. Freeways had replaced the game trail, and the tribe was focused on roadside casinos, not salmon runs. Norman insisted that winning money from moss eaters, although satisfying, didn't make you any less subjugated. *Those who forsake the old ways are fools who have sold their own hearts.* The old ways meant little to Leland; he lived in a doublewide and bought his food from a grocery store. Still the old man persisted: *The salmon are a part of us.*

The sun grew closer to the foothills toward the west, and Leland knelt at the edge. He shoved the post into pale green water a half foot out, struggling against the current to keep it in place. When he felt the soft silt and gravel of the river bottom give beneath the timber's butt, he slowly rose, placing his boot on the post to hold it steady. With his boot he angled the post back to the nearest crossbeam. Then Leland took the sledge and drove the post deeper into the river bottom. Once it was stable, he secured the leg to the frame with a pair of long nails and repeated the process on the other side of the brace. With the legs in place, he resumed planking the expanding deck.

In the distance, Leland heard the shrill cry of a train's whistle. He looked up from his work, wondering whether the train was headed east or west. A car paused on the bridge, idling, before it continued on toward Highway 14. Probably checking his progress before reporting back to Hood River. Leland watched the road until the car was out of sight.

Throughout the afternoon and into the early evening he pieced together the sections, framing and then overlaying the slats. When the deck was complete, there was nothing left to build but the overhead scaffolding. The single archway, placed near the center of the walkway, would be used to help hoist the large nets from the water.

With the platform rebuilt, Leland walked back to the shore. The boards creaked beneath his boots. He retrieved a salmon carcass and a jar of eggs from the small cooler, and the sage grass braid and lighter from his jacket pocket. The sun was low in the sky, painting the horizon pink. Leland stretched his back, arms and legs; this wasn't how he'd hoped to spend the weekend. Normally he would sleep in, before going downtown to the Snag to have a few beers, play darts, and watch the Blazers game.

The carcass he freed in the shallow waters near the shore, an offering to show his people's respect for the salmon. It drifted quietly over the gravel. He lit the sage grass and slowly waved the smoldering braid over the structure. Norman claimed the smoke would purify and protect the wood from bad spirits. Leland grimaced, noting that the smoke hadn't saved the first platform from destruction earlier that week. Once the sacred smoke had touched every inch, the braid was left to smolder on the rocks at the entrance. The small fire would invite Coyote to sate his ferocious appetite from the narrow river.

He noticed someone was watching the ceremony now from the end of the bridge, but Leland was running out of daylight. He smeared the little red eggs on the legs where they met the water, to encourage the salmon to remember these forsaken spawning grounds. The final step of the ceremony, Norman told his grandson, was the most important. In the scaffolding, Leland hung a willow branch to recognize Coyote's ingenuity, and his generosity in teaching the people to fish. He secured the branch with the twine traditionally used to make nets.

Leland didn't believe in these charms, but now he wouldn't have to lie when Norman asked if he had anointed the platform. He surveyed his work from the shore. The old man had provided the spiritual instructions, but the deck and dock construction were based on modern techniques researched at the Stevenson Public Library. He stepped roughly on the center of the walkway and bounced. Shock waves passed through the planks, reverberating out to the pale green pool and quickly disappearing in the swirling current. Barring a flash flood, or human intervention, the platform should last through fishing season.

The sunlight was fading, and the temperature began to drop. Leland returned his canvas jacket to his shoulders. Suddenly he felt hungry; he had consumed little beyond coffee and beef jerky, and his stomach rumbled and churned like the water below the falls. Although no one was standing by the bridge now, Leland sensed someone nearby.

He picked up a few spare beams, and headed up the embankment. At the turn around, a silver Subaru Forester with Oregon plates was pulled up close to the bridge. The roof rack held a kayak and a roof box. The box was covered with stickers with phrases like *My Other Car Is A Mountain Bike,* and *Rafters Do It In The Water.* Leland thought of the stickers on Norman's truck: *Insured by Smith and Wesson, Seattle SuperSonics* and his latest, an Indian Brave holding a sign that read *Unoccupy America.* Leland's truck was free of stickers. There was nothing he wanted to broadcast to the rest of the world. And working in the garage, he'd seen the damage those vinyl vanities could inflict on a paint job.

Inside the car, the driver watched as Leland made several trips to stow the remaining planks. Even in the twilight, he recognized the man behind the wheel. Josh Sanders ran more boats down the White Salmon than any of the other eight outfitters. Leland had never met Sanders, but he'd seen his picture in the paper and on the local stations during the hearings. Although his arguments were not clever, Sanders was aggressive during the hearings: *The Yakama haven't shown any interest in the White Salmon for generations. But now that the river is truly valuable, after we invested in it for decades, they want to cash in. Their platforms will obstruct the river and hurt the local economy. We aren't the ones asking for special treatment. We just want to know why they can't fish from shore like everybody else?* The crowd behind him had cheered, as he flashed a big toothy grin.

Sanders exited his SUV. He had broad oarsman shoulders, but stood a good head shorter than Leland. He guessed Sanders was in his mid 20s, but it was hard to tell, as the neatly trimmed brown beard made him look older. As Sanders watched intently, Leland stowed the last of his tools and the cooler, and firmly shut the tailgate.

The young entrepreneur continued to stare across the turnaround at Leland, and then slowly moved his gaze down toward the water. His eyes were the cold slate of a river rock, worn smooth by the water, and possessed a calm, confident quality. Sanders appeared to be waiting, and he was in no hurry to move.

Leland paused half way to the truck's cab. He wondered if Sanders would have the gall to walk down there and destroy his work after being seen. Sanders continued to wait patiently by the Subaru. Leland felt the urge to knock the self-assured half smile from that smug face. For a moment the two men locked eyes, Sanders's river rocks and Leland's dark as silt. Stubborn pride forced out Leland's most stoic glare. Sanders was daring him to leave the platform unattended.

Leland wished that there was something in the cooler besides raw salmon eggs. Norman's shotgun idea suddenly seemed appealing. He leaned against the hood, arms folded across his chest. "You know," Leland said, "I shot an elk in these woods once. Big old bull, a five-point, stood up in a thicket just a little farther from me than you're standing now. Caught him clean in the chest."

"I don't know what the hell you're talking about," said Sanders.

"Didn't think you would." Leland smiled and entered his pickup, rolled the window down. He turned the key, just enough to power the radio, and listened to the second half of the basketball game. Above the static and play-by-play, he could hear the crunch of gravel as Sanders paced back and forth. The sun vanished; another train called out from down in the Gorge. Coyotes answered the train with yips of laughter from the foothills. Leland didn't budge.

In the darkness, Sanders slammed the door of the Subaru, and peeled out onto the road, spitting gravel in his wake. Leland flipped the key from accessory to start, and the old pickup sputtered to life. Go ahead and tear it down, Leland thought as he drove off. He'd rebuild it, as many times as it took.

In Spite of All the Danger

The first time I discounted the achievements of Roberto Mancini was the first time I saw him. I was stuck at the Sacramento Airport, and his picture stared boldly from page E2 of the *Sentinel*. His jaw held firm, brow furled above black eyes narrowed with concentration. He was dressed in a black and red Neoprene suit, with dark slicked back hair and a twirled mustache.

Mancini's mustache reminded me of pictures of my great uncle, Chester "Pinky" Hager. A railroad worker, Pinky was so boisterous and opinionated that Grandpa said even his Unitarian congregation couldn't stand to be near him. Grandpa thought that was hilarious, a Unitarian excommunicated. Although I never met the man, Pinky looked like an individual full of swagger. A cocky smile peeked from beneath that twirled mustache and his stare was direct. And in all of the photographs, his fists held his suspenders. He looked like the sort who'd challenge you to a bare-knuckle boxing match. A hardnosed union representative, Pinky never shied away from personal risk. Mancini's mustache and countenance projected the same confident air, but that wasn't the reason I belittled him.

I arrived at the airport that day to learn my flight had been cancelled. I'd spent a long weekend visiting some friends who'd started their own advertising firm in the Bay area after our Seattle office downsized. Actually, their office was in Modesto but the Bay area sounded more appealing to investors. At the time, they'd asked me to join them in California but the risk seemed too high. Leaving meant dragging Karen away from her family and abandoning our support system in Washington. And while we could no longer afford our place in Ballard on a single income, Karen had a connection at OHSU that got her a job in transcription. With the cost of housing considerably less across the river in Vancouver, it made sense to make the move. How could I ask her to pass up a sure thing? Despite all that, I wished she'd shown more faith to take the risk with me. My friends spent the weekend ribbing me for being gutless. I defended my decision by comparing crime rates and the cost of living. But my excuses about the opportunities in Portland despite the recession, and the connections I was racking up teaching at Vancouver WorkSource, rang false even to me. Fortunately, they didn't belabor the point. Still I was glad I went. The firm was finally stable, and I hadn't seen them in over two years.

Karen spent the weekend at the hospital, catching up on paperwork. When she dropped me off Thursday night she mentioned it'd been almost a year since we'd spent a weekend away together.

At the desk, the booking agents were vague about the reason for the cancellation, something about the plane "never arriving" in Sacramento. They made it sound like the whole plane was misplaced. I was supposed to infer that the airline had found some mechanical problem and grounded the plane, for safety reasons. In reality, I suspected that a glance at the paltry number of passengers convinced them the flight wasn't worth their time or money.

Everyone was booked on the next flight with a speed and efficiency that confirmed my suspicions. The only other direct flight to Portland that Monday night was on a competitor's plane, two and a half hours later. That flight must've been equally empty, since rebooking the entire load was no trouble. My friends, of course, had dropped me at the terminal more than an hour before the scheduled departure. They didn't park, didn't get out and didn't look back.

As reparation, all displaced passengers were given an $8.00 voucher for food. Good at any of the restaurants clustered around the terminal, but not valid for the purchase of alcohol. The airline was obviously afraid of the dangers posed by a plane half full of disgruntled passengers, intoxicated by the one stiff drink that eight dollars would buy in an airport cocktail lounge.

With little choice, I entered the twisting labyrinth of black straps to security. Once through, I called Karen to let her know about the delay and when to pick me up at PDX. At the intersection of the silver and white halls of the terminals, I stood and listened to her moan about the delay and how she had to get up early. Her tone implied that I should feel guilty for this inconvenience. I wasn't exactly thrilled about getting in at midnight either. But even though I wasn't responsible for the cancelled flight, I still apologized, added that I loved her and would call once on the ground.

It was amazing how much modern airports resembled the shopping malls of my youth. Climate controlled indoor environments where I could buy anything, from a last-minute haircut or meal to a magazine or gum for the flight. I considered getting Karen some sort of gift, a Sacramento sweatshirt or shot glass. But no random trinket would appease her once she'd decided to remain angry.

Near the end of the sterile hallway, I found the gate where the new flight would depart. Everything looked to be in order, with slightly cushioned chairs, welded together as benches and arranged around a central podium for the ticket taker. The seats were littered with travelers in various states of transition. Some, I could tell, had been on the move for a while, probably changed several time zones, gained and lost days. They were sacked out on the short benches or drowsed in isolated chairs. Others, bright eyed, had probably only been at the airport for 45 minutes. They yammered away on cell phones with friends they'd soon visit, or family they'd just left. A few fathers anxiously marched their children up and down the terminal in an attempt to keep the little ones from annoying those around them. These men, with their worn sunken-eyed looks, shuffled slowly down the corridor like zombies, uninterested in the living around them.

I adjusted the strap of the duffle bag on my shoulder and turned back toward the row of shops and cafes. I wasn't hungry, but if I didn't use the voucher the airline would somehow go unpunished. $8.00 wasn't a lot for a dinner, especially with the captive audience rule in effect. Airport vendors, ski resorts and theme parks all realize their prices can be unreasonable. Secure in the knowledge that if you want it and didn't bring it, you aren't getting it anywhere else. I set the goal of getting something solely with the voucher without spending any extra cash.

I found a restaurant with several menu items priced below eight dollars. The place looked like a nightclub had collided with a neighborhood bistro. The décor was slick and ultra modern, with low lighting and faux brick walls, everything trimmed in chrome. A flat screen in the far corner flashed soccer highlights; Greece had been eliminated by the Czech Republic from the Euro Cup. The screen was filled with happy Czech supporters. They sang and formed a human chain with their arms around one another's shoulders as they jumped and swayed back and forth in the stands. I could only imagine the announcer's smarmy commentary about the match with Greece involving bounced Czechs. I took a seat on a black vinyl bench, my bag in the chair across the table. I verified the place would take the voucher and ordered a house salad with a glass of lemon water, $6.45.

The TV shifted to coverage of baseball. My cell phone was out on the table, but no one called. A woman in her early 20s came in, chatting with a girl about 13-years-old. They took the corner table at the end of the row. After several minutes of asking the waitress for recommendations, they ignored them and decided to split a burger and mozzarella sticks. Then came their drink orders, a pair of virgin margaritas. The girl beamed; the whole setting must have seemed so glamorous and exciting. She was included in the adult world for once. The woman appeared less impressed but hid it well from the girl. I wondered what her relationship was to the teen. Aunt? Sister? Cousin?

Over the speakers, I could scarcely make out a piano version of "It's Only a Paper Moon," one of Karen's favorites. We'd played the Ella Fitzgerald version at our wedding reception. I remembered swinging her out across the dance floor. We'd spent three months at a dance studio on Capitol Hill learning the Lindy Hop. I never did get the hang of leading. Our friends and relatives enveloped us as she stepped in toward me, swaying her hips beneath her gown, and mouthing the lyrics: "Yes, its only a canvas sky;

Hanging over a muslin tree; But it wouldn't be make-believe if you believed in me." And I was struck by how the simple melody lost something without the lyrics. I finished my salad and left two dollars on the table for the waitress, assuming the restaurant would pocket the extra cash from the voucher.

Down the hall, I perused a magazine kiosk. Tabloids, sports journals, and fashion magazines were placed on the most prominent shelves. Steroid infused men grimaced while flexing swollen biceps, next to waifish models and the latest celebrity shame (some starlet topless, a senator snorting cocaine off a stripper's breast). Another shelf was filled with mass-market paperback novels. Romances, detective stories, and spy thrillers, the sort of thing I never read, but Karen adored. I generally made it a rule to only read books that had been around for at least ten years. After settling on a newspaper, I headed back to the gate.

The seating area was deserted. The handful of leftover travelers were probably from the cancelled flight, back from using their vouchers. Most of the gates around the terminal were empty, as the evening flights steadily departed. I took a seat apart from the small group and near the windows.

As I flipped through the paper nothing really caught my eye until the arts and entertainment section. The headline on E2 read: "Man Crosses Niagara Falls on Tight Rope." And there he was, a quarter page action hero: Roberto Mancini. Initially the prospect thrilled me. This daring act was the sort of thing I romanticized as a kid when I wanted to grow up and train whales. An audacious feat that required nerves of steel.

In the picture, Roberto Mancini's left hand clutched a long pole to his waist; a strap around his neck vertically suspended the pole. With his right hand he pointed straight ahead, indicating his path, as if he had a choice. His eyes were intense, focused on his footing. He stood suspended over a gray void of mist.

The rope wasn't a thin tight strand like you'd see at the circus. This was a substantial cable, to account for the sag over that distance, the weight of the rope itself, and the amount of condensation that inevitably covered its surface. The story explained the technical problems, and that Roberto Mancini was the grandson of the famous Magnificent Mancinis. This family of acrobats astounded the United States with feats like climbing the Empire State Building, and tight rope walks between buildings in the 1930s and 40s. The article was as much a profile of the Magnificent Mancinis as it was a description of Roberto's stunt.

Roberto Mancini was the first person to cross the gorge in 116 years and the first ever to pass directly above the falls. It took him around 30 minutes to cross into Canada. But then the article provided the detail that killed my interest: while Roberto couldn't employ a net, he was secured with a harness. In the picture, I now saw the second cable hanging down like a tail behind him, fastened to the rope by a strong metal ring.

As soon as I read about the harness, I no longer cared about Roberto Mancini or his walk. And I knew I wouldn't look into his next exploit, a similar walk across the Grand Canyon. I closed the paper in disgust and walked toward the end of the terminal.

Outside the sun was setting. The sky was a vibrant aqua blue with streaks of pink. The terminal was quiet. Other flights arrived, their passengers marching off without a second glance at the terminal refugees. The air would briefly fill with the sound of their cellphone chatter, before the noise level ebbed back into a calm stillness.

My flight seemed to be the last one departing that evening. Gradually the number of travelers increased. Segregated around the gate, it was easy to pick out which passengers had not planned on taking this particular flight. Their faces were wilted from the monotony of waiting. Time, usually so precious, had become our collective enemy.

I leaned against one of the posts between the massive windows that made up the outer walls and watched clouds pass by. The clouds seemed to be outlined in black, like cardboard cutouts suspended against a sheet sky in a school auditorium. All I could think about was Mancini, and how he'd cheated me, like a kid breaking pre-sawed boards in a grade school talent show. But why? Why did the safety precaution make such a big difference? I didn't want Roberto Mancini to fall to his death. But I did want him to risk death for me. To acknowledge the risk, and, in spite of all the danger, still decide to try. The harness made the feat less impressive, less thrilling.

If someone said: *Why don't you cross that cable over Niagara Falls?* My answer would be a definite no. I wouldn't give it a second thought. But if the same person explained that I would be safely strapped on---well, I still wouldn't attempt the walk, but I would at least give it a little more consideration. So why was I disappointed in Roberto, when I would make the same choice?

The harness didn't make the crossing less difficult. Still, somehow it cheapened his accomplishment. I pictured college students slack-lining between the trees in Esther

Short Park. When their arms began to flail for balance they would simply step down, the drooping line only a foot off the ground. The harness put Mancini on their level. Without the risk to him, there was no reward for me.

At the gate, the ticket takers began to assemble by the podium. The fresh-faced passengers who had just arrived would be the first permitted to board. That felt unjust to those who had waited, camped out near the gate for so long. As I walked back toward the gate, I texted Karen that the flight was leaving soon. Then crumpled Roberto Mancini into a ball and dumped him into a trashcan.

From This Day

LeAnn didn't need an alarm clock; Achilles woke her at five every morning with his whining. He paced back and forth at the foot of the brass bed, nails clicking on the wood floor. If she didn't get up right away, he'd paw the door, deepening grooves he'd already created. Or worse, Achilles would grab the sheets with his slobbering mouth, pulling them back from her side of the bed.

But that Saturday morning, LeAnn was already awake, before the pawing or the whining. Lying in bed, she listened to the rain pat the window above the headboard. The languid rhythm imposed a dull hum on the flaps of the vents. Her eyes drifted in and out of focus, mapping the shadowy bumps across the plastered ceiling, when they weren't fixed on Megan.

Megan was still asleep, sprawled on her stomach, occupying more than her side of the bed. Chestnut hair tousled just above the collar of her Timbers' jersey. Achilles wouldn't pester her. Walking him was LeAnn's job. Megan looked peaceful, oblivious to the hurt she had caused, or the confusion and doubts that crowded LeAnn's thoughts.

Let her walk the dog, LeAnn thought, as Achilles stretched to begin his morning routine. Achilles slept at the foot of their bed, but favored Megan's side. LeAnn supposed he recognized that she was the reason he was with them. LeAnn never claimed to be a dog person and an aging greyhound with a bladder problem was not her idea of a good pet. She was, however, a Megan person. And Megan had her heart set on rescuing a greyhound after she volunteered at the Humane Society. She told LeAnn how greyhounds had the sweetest temperament of any dog breed. And how they were worthless to racetracks once they hit three years old. With these facts alone, she'd agreed to adopt Achilles, sight unseen, and LeAnn had gone along, assumptions unchallenged.

Despite her irritation, LeAnn got up before their tan greyhound could start his complaints to take him for his morning walk and piss. She stumbled through her five am routine, getting dressed in the darkened bedroom, trying her best not to wake Megan. She threw on track pants, a sweatshirt from her dresser, and grabbed her purple rain jacket. All the while Achilles continued to paw at the door, occasionally yipping or snapping his teeth when she opened a drawer, or made another trip to the bathroom for ChapStick or a headband.

In the pocket of her jacket, LeAnn felt the slight mass of the ring box on her hip. That's right, she thought, today we were supposed to be celebrating. She glared at Megan, who rolled over. She felt the smooth, soft black velvet upholstery of the box with her fingertips and sighed.

The night before, they'd finished the leftover take-out Thai food from two days earlier. LeAnn was cleaning up after cooking dinner for Achilles. Megan was watching the evening news. Same-sex marriage licenses would be offered at the county courthouse for the first time at midnight. Couples had already started lining up to get one. LeAnn put the last of the dishes away and went to their bedroom. On the screen as she passed, she recognized Stephan and Ryan, the Clark County organizers, in matching tuxedos.

She'd stashed the ring in her sock drawer. She slipped into a simple red dress, Megan's favorite color on her. At the full-length mirror on the closet door she combed her short blonde hair and smoothed her dress. Satisfied, she looked good enough to be potentially caught by news cameras. She put on her jacket and slipped the ring box into her pocket.

When she returned to the living room, Achilles had curled up with Megan on the couch. LeAnn made a space for herself on her other side. As they shifted their bodies on the couch, Achilles bared his teeth and made a low growl. But he forgot his agitation once he was able to settle his head in Megan's lap.

Megan looked at her jacket. "Going somewhere?"

"Let's go to the courthouse," LeAnn said.

"What for?"

She could feel the ring box resting on her upper thigh. "I thought we could get a marriage license."

Megan laughed. "Are you asking me to elope?"

"We don't have to use it right away. We have 60 days to decide." Megan's amused expression didn't change. "Or we could wait. Spring or maybe August would be nice."

"You're serious."

LeAnn smiled and nodded.

Megan placed her hand on LeAnn's leg. "I don't want to get married."

For a moment, they sat in silence. As Megan studied the ten-day forecast, her hand absently held LeAnn's leg. LeAnn studied the side of her partner's face, expectant of something more. She noticed the dog's smug stare.

She brushed the hand off her thigh, onto the dog's muzzle. Rising slowly, she stood between Megan and the screen. Achilles curled his lip and showed his yellow teeth.

"Then why get so worked up about marriage equality?"

Megan stroked Achilles's head until he relaxed again. She shrugged. "Just because I don't believe in something doesn't mean I can't support the rights of others."

LeAnn was dumbstruck. She and Megan had been together for nearly eight years. When they moved into this apartment together six years ago, they took turns carrying each other over the threshold. Megan had been quick to volunteer to help the initiative coalition. Week after week, they'd gone door-to-door gathering signatures. Competing to see who could get the most, Megan exhilarated when she came out on top. As the election approached, she worked the phones every evening.

LeAnn assumed they'd never discussed marriage before because it wasn't an option. She never dreamed they wouldn't be on the same page.

She narrowed her eyes at Megan. Studied her expression. Wondered if this could be some kind of joke. "That's stupid."

Megan let the insult pass. She pulled her hair back and reached for LeAnn's hand. "I don't need the state to validate what we have."

"The hell with the state. Do it for us...for me."

"It won't change our relationship. You'll still be overly organized and sensitive. I'll still be scattered and work strange hours." Megan stood and pulled LeAnn into an embrace she didn't return. "I don't need a piece of paper to remind me to make this work." She ran her fingers through LeAnn's hair. "We both know the majority of marriages end in divorce."

LeAnn pushed back, held Megan at arm's length. "But we aren't them."

A silence fell over the room. Megan returned to the couch with Achilles, while LeAnn continued to stand in front of the muted TV.

"I'm sorry. It's nothing personal." Megan finally offered.

LeAnn had retreated to the bedroom and changed into pajama pants and a t-shirt. She hung her jacket back in the closet. In the living room the sound came back on the TV. They didn't speak the rest of the night.

LeAnn grabbed her keys and stepped into the rubber boots with pink anchors Megan had given her for her birthday. Megan rolled and moaned in response to the chime of the keys.

LeAnn grabbed Achilles's front legs and strapped on his faux coyote fur coat. Personally, she found greyhounds homely with their gangly bodies. There was a stretch of fur that ran across Achilles's ribs, patchy and scarred, from the time that he tried to leave the track midrace. The pattern left by the railing gave him the appearance of wearing grotesque racing stripes painted across his flesh.

He snapped at her hands as she slid the matching snood over his head. In the coat he looked a good five pounds heavier, bushy and rotund. Megan had bought the coat and snood to celebrate Achilles's first anniversary. LeAnn had just barely managed to talk her out of purchasing the matching galoshes at the doggie boutique. In her mind, the only positive of the coat was that it concealed his scars. She muzzled and leashed Achilles, who was suddenly reluctant to leave Megan. As she dragged him out of the bedroom he pulled against the leash, snarling, his nails scratching the wood floor.

Finally outside, LeAnn and Achilles followed a short gravel walk to the bike path that ran along the Columbia just south of their building. Achilles sniffed his way along, stopping regularly at large rocks and clumps of decorative grass. If a site were deemed worthy, he would linger to lift a scrawny leg. The morning was cold and wet, like most this time of year in Vancouver. If the dog noticed, he didn't mind, as he was in no hurry. Honestly, LeAnn wondered, how many times do you have to mark the same rock before the world knew it belonged to you?

A steady drizzle drummed against the hood of her rain jacket as she waited for him. In the distance only a handful of cars crossed the I-5 Bridge into Portland in the early morning light. Achilles lifted his leg by a piece of bleached driftwood, placed next to the path for decoration. The white branch bore multiple yellow stains from his rivals. But at this point in the walk he was out of piss, and his action was more for show, in case other dogs were watching. After a few minutes, LeAnn nudged his hindquarters with the toe of her boot. He looked back at her with unconcealed contempt and they continued down the path.

LeAnn shivered and held the lead tight, since at this point in the walk the temperamental dog often decided to run. Her knuckles were white and rough, the fleshy parts of her hands perpetually bandaged. Only after the adoption papers were signed, she learned that Achilles had demonstrated consistent antisocial behavior since he was a puppy. He would growl and lunge at other dogs like a surly ex-boxer, always trying to pick a fight at the bar. His aggression wasn't reserved for the other dogs in the kennel. Achilles lashed out at his handlers and trainers, baring his teeth at anything on two legs, except Megan.

The dog nips, LeAnn told her coworkers, the first time they examined her bandaged hands. They shook their heads and told her that bites, not nips, drew blood. But LeAnn continued to put on a brave face, trying to convince them it was all done out of affection. Yeah, she thought, the dog bites me because he likes me. Consequently, none of their friends or coworkers had been to their apartment in years.

Megan rescued Achilles three years ago from the Multnomah Greyhound Park when his racing career was over. Achilles was retired early, having failed his initial trials. He lacked interest in chasing the lure. LeAnn couldn't blame him. Who would want that moldy stuffed rabbit?

Megan became obsessed with making his life meaningful, just like she did with all of her causes. Whether it was a girl's school in Afghanistan, or winter coats for foster kids, no injustice was too great or small for Megan. If Achilles had issues, that just made him all the more appealing. That sense of righteousness, of commitment, despite the virtue signaling that accompanied it, was one of the things that first attracted LeAnn to her. The thought of Megan and last night made her tear up.

To distract herself, LeAnn contemplated what would need to be done once they returned from their walk. First, she would have to cook Achilles breakfast. His poor disposition was compounded with severe allergies. He couldn't eat regular dog food without getting sick. No matter the brand or quality they tried, he puked all over the apartment, staining and matting the beige carpets. After multiple visits and numerous tests, the vet instructed Megan to cook him a simple starch and lean meat. But Megan didn't know how to cook, so the task fell to LeAnn.

This time-consuming chore was also the ultimate joke. She cooked for the dog more than she'd ever cooked for them as a couple. Megan would rather eat out or order in.

And if cooking for Achilles wasn't enough, his diet had to be varied. After a month of eating a particular meat just fine, he'd develop a new allergy and the retching would begin again.

That month, LeAnn had spent her evenings riding the light rail out to several butchers in Beaverton and Hillsboro to get cuts of kangaroo. If anyone else had told her they put out that kind of effort for a dog, she would've told them they were crazy. But Megan loved Achilles, so LeAnn boiled his potatoes, ground his pills, and rounded up as many different types of meat as she could find.

Near the base of the bridge, Achilles and LeAnn came to the end of the path. He nosed around the chain link fence that kept them from going under the bridge. She wondered if Megan would be up by now, and hoped she was still sleeping. If LeAnn could just get dressed for the day and Achilles fed, she could avoid the scene simmering inside.

LeAnn clicked her tongue and tugged on his leash. They began the walk back home, stopping to sniff and check the bits of territory already marked on their walk. Every once in a while, Achilles dug deep, found a little piss in the recesses of his bladder, perhaps freshly generated from a drink in a puddle, and managed to mark a stone or log of particular importance to him.

In her pocket, LeAnn stroked the ring box. The ring had one decent sized diamond, set in white gold. The Rhodium plated band was sculpted into a rope pattern, with four smaller diamonds placed in the entwined sections, two on either side of the main stone. It had belonged to her grandmother.

When LeAnn first came out, she was unsure how her grandparents would react. Her grandfather was a stern, conservative, retired merchant marine and longshoreman. To say that lesbian and gay were pejorative terms in Longview would be an understatement. Most people there would use different, coarser words to describe her. When she finally told them, her grandfather remained silent. After a few minutes, he made an excuse about needing to pick up salt for the water softener before walking out of the house. Her grandmother held her, stroked her hair, and told LeAnn that it didn't matter.

For years after that day, the two of them had never mentioned her sexuality again. Her grandfather didn't treat LeAnn any differently, except he stopped asking when she was going to get married.

LeAnn had visited him two weeks prior, after the initiative had passed. She never talked politics with her grandfather. They sat in his living room, Grandmother's empty chair between them. He showed her a clipping from the *Columbian* that featured a picture of her standing with Megan on a street corner in Vancouver, holding up signs in favor of the initiative. He seemed hurt that she hadn't told him about their involvement.

He rose from his chair, just as he had the day she told them. Walked toward the door, but didn't leave this time. Instead he opened a small drawer in the roll top desk and produced the ring box. With quivering hands he gave it to her. "Your Gram would've wanted you to have it," he said. He released her hand and returned to his chair.

LeAnn didn't know what to say and told him as much. He shrugged and told her, "Just make sure you give it to someone who deserves you."

Achilles paused at yet another rock, and she nearly tripped as her shin bumped against his side. He yelped as she jerked back to the present and kept herself from falling. The morning fog was beginning to lift in patches. She could see a marina across the river. The boats were clustered together, tucked away from the open water by the arms of the dock.

Back at the apartment, once the door was closed behind them, she removed Achilles's muzzle and leash. He trotted off toward the bedroom, where Megan was thankfully still asleep. LeAnn approached with caution, hoping to pick out her clothes for the day without startling them. As she entered the room, Achilles turned, crouching low to the ground and baring his teeth. LeAnn wanted to scream: *Just five minutes ago I was your pal. Remember, I helped you out, you bastard.* She inched along the wall, not getting too close. Atop her dresser she found his rope toy. She wanted to grab the coarse knot and smack him across the face and hear him yelp as his slight frame collapsed to the floor. But she didn't.

She should pack her clothes. Feed Achilles a scoop of *Purina* and leave the puke for Megan to clean up. But where could she go? And she had no other reason to doubt Megan's commitment. If nothing else had changed, was a piece of paper really worth leaving over?

Achilles suddenly grabbed the rope in his mouth and began to tussle the toy with vigor. The force jerked her arm back and forth. She pulled back, trying to yank the rope from his mouth. LeAnn and Achilles engaged in their tug of war, both straining to release their frustration, while Megan slept.

Zombie Bees

Near Ruby Junction, I boarded the last car of the Blue Line and took a seat at the back. The shiny plastic of the Bombardier's shell was meant to look futuristic, or sterilized. But years of use and the futile cleaning of occasional vandalism had left the train's interior dull. Or maybe it was the way I looked at things.

The car was sparsely populated. I had the whole backbench and raised area to myself. The center was occupied by several hipsters, ear buds jammed into their skulls and noses glued to cell phones, androgynous in their tight pants and big glasses. They avoided eye contact with the other passengers. Watching them, I was reminded of how all the latest music fads and slang had passed me by. Once I'd been the one my friends sought for insight on the latest band. I felt envious of their isolated self-confidence and wondered if my angry adolescent days were over.

It was the first night I'd ventured out of my apartment in over a month, since Lucille left. Devin had invited me to a jazz club on 10th Avenue. He'd called rather than texted to ensure I got the invite. Insisted I had to hear the club's house band. That they were phenomenal, led by an old Motown session drummer. And best of all, he told me, there was no cover charge. It wasn't the sort of place we used to hang out and I couldn't tell if the invitation was based on pity. But even though I was reluctant to go, I didn't want to dampen Devin's excitement.

I got off the Blue Line at Goose Hollow station, ignoring the more convenient Galleria stop where Lucille and I'd first kissed, and made my way through the Pearl District. That kiss was on our first date, a week after she'd safely delivered Devin and me back to our apartment, along with a large pizza, breadsticks and a two liter bottle of Mountain Dew. She'd taken me to a show that featured some of her urns at PSU. We'd gotten a few drinks after, and both of us had a good buzz. I remember how the damp pavement shone beneath the street lamps. She leaned against a lamppost and smiled at me, and I asked her what she was thinking. She said, "I'm wondering if you're ever going to kiss me." And that was all the encouragement I needed.

I hadn't been out on the town in years. Not since our band Animatronic Cowboy broke up. After Morgan, our lead singer and chief songwriter, told us he was moving to Seattle to form a new band, I punched the warehouse wall in frustration. I broke my left hand and couldn't play guitar anymore. Without a singer or a lead guitar player with nimble fingers, Animatronic Cowboy quickly dissolved. I quit barhopping and playing music with Devin, and settled into a quiet routine with Lucille. A routine I thought she enjoyed. She had never expressed a strong interest in our music. "You play the same songs every night. I've heard them," she'd say after a string of excuses about being tired or having other commitments.

After I broke my hand, it was a non-issue. We went to art galleries and occasionally hung around for an after party. Most of the time we stayed in, cooked simple meals for each other and listened to music. She always thought her records were better, or at least more authentic, than mine. Whatever that meant.

I followed the labyrinth of narrow one-way streets as they wound past the familiar facades of faded brick buildings. Some now housed boutiques, restaurants, used bookstores and coffee houses. Others remained boarded up, abandoned in spite of the Pearl's rebirth into the trendy part of the city.

At the corner I waited for the light to change and stared through a bright window display of expensive shoes with foreign names. The labels meant little to me, but I'm sure they would have impressed Lucille. I realized that these shelves of shoes had replaced pool tables and stalls of the first pub I entered legally. Devin and I were already pretty far gone by the time we hit this place, having started the party in our apartment with cheaper spirits purchased at the neighborhood liquor store. Red cheeked and leaning against each other, we staggered up to the bar.

When the owner learned it was my birthday, he didn't offer me a free shot. At that point in the evening, he probably figured I'd had enough. Instead, he invited us down to the basement to see the Shanghai tunnels that run under the older parts of town. The tunnel's entrance breathed a dank breeze, accented with the slight stench of mold and rat shit. I stared into its perfect darkness through the cracks of the board-covered door. That was the sort of darkness you could disappear in. But the shoe store looked warm and clean, incompatible with my memories of the tunnel.

The light turned and the white walk hand beckoned me to cross. I continued toward the club, drawn on by its neon sign. My legs felt shaky beneath my weight. I'd never been to this club before. Unsure of the decorum I decided not to wear the clothes of the past, ripped jeans and a work shirt.

Instead, I wore my black suit with a white shirt. I passed on a tie, but carried a thin one in my pocket just in case. I hadn't worn this suit since Lucille's sister's wedding, two years prior. The jacket fit fine, but the pants felt snug at the waist.

Outside the club, I sat on a bike rack and waited for Devin. A red neon saxophone shined above the entrance. I studied my reflection in the wide front windows. Deliberately, I rubbed the palm of my hand along my cheek and down my chin, as though I were wiping my mouth. The skin was smooth, but just that morning my face had been covered with a coarse beard.

I had stopped shaving when I locked myself away. I made few excursions outside, only to the convenience store across the street. I frequented the store at unusual hours, so the clerk would usually be the only person I had to interact with. With my ratty appearance, I could tell I made the clerk uneasy, unsure of what I might do. It reminded me of the suspicious looks we used to get when Devin wore his red Mohawk and I wore my hair in two braids, one green and one blue, grinning as we presented our fake IDs.

I didn't normally wear a beard, so my reflection in the window resembled me more than the face in this morning's mirror. In movies, depressed men always stopped shaving. So, how do bearded men physically manifest their depression? Or were they just always depressed? I'd considered this as I lathered my face and breathed in the steam from the sink. Wasn't Lincoln melancholy, I thought, as I slowly dragged the razor across my face, savoring the warm water, the slight tug of the blades against the resistant hair.

Once finished, I splashed water on my face and stared into the mirror. The image that met my gaze was pale and emaciated. Big puffy bags sunk my eyes deep into their sockets. I placed my hands on either side of the sink and leaned in toward the mirror. Beneath my left palm, I fingered the razor. How easy it would be to slit my wrist. I imagined the lines carved into my forearm. Crooked and branching out like a tree. Or maybe the gashes would form a "Y" like two rivers converging on a map. Yes, the cold, red confluence of the Willamette and the Columbia, dripping down my arm.

I narrowed my eyes and breathed deep the thick air. I'd have to be sure. I knew no one would appear to rescue me. Devin wouldn't have thought anything if I hadn't shown up that night. The cuts would be a real act, not some desperate plea for attention. I laughed when I thought of what the paramedics would find, when they finally came in search of me. Sleeping pills littered the desk. There was a clock on the wall of each room and another on each flat surface, aside from the bathroom counter. I'd appear to be a man obsessed with time. But I couldn't afford any screw-ups; I wasn't looking to suffer. Finally, I shook my head and threw the razor on the floor.

Devin snuck up on me, slapping the back of my head. "I was starting to think you'd died," he said and we engaged in a half-hearted embrace before entering the club. The room was all dark hardwood, the floors merging with the tables, the bar, and the doors. The walls were painted a muted mustard. Candles and red pendant fixtures lit the room with a dull glow. Devin led the way to a table by the windows, three back from the stage.

I sat with my back to the window. Devin was turned sideways to the table, facing the front of the room. He ordered a hummus plate and two Widmer Hefeweizen. His hands rested on the table, sliding the ashtray back and forth between them. Between the noise of the crowded room and his fidgeting I began to feel anxious, trapped.

A small stage was set up at the front of the room, with a red curtain for a backdrop. Simple, but far more elegant than the venues we'd typically played, makeshift stages crammed in the corner of a bar or a friend's basement. Thursdays here featured the quartet version of the house band: drums, guitar, alto saxophone and a bass.

Devin and I still worked together, as orderlies at Good Shepard Hospital. Lucille found me the job after I broke my hand, thought a regular schedule would be good for me. I'd been in to work only once the past month. After I'd spent five hours mopping the same square of tile, the ward nurse sent me home. I got the impression Devin was tired of picking up the slack. I didn't hold that against him. Regardless of his other motives, he wanted me to get on with my life. Considering that I had already burned through my vacation and sick time, and was running a serious risk of being fired, that was good advice.

Devin was the first to swear that Lucille was a bitch after she left with that photographer for Oklahoma City. "With any luck a tornado will drop a house on her," he said, slapping the back of my head that first day at the hospital. Even though I knew he was right, I clenched my hands around the mop handle, kept my mouth shut and my eyes on the floor. He yammered at me for another few minutes, declaring I was better off, before getting back to avoiding his own work.

The waitress brought our beers. She placed the hummus platter at the center of the table and a small plate in front of each of us. "What exactly happened?" Devin asked as he dipped a piece of pita in the hummus and took a bite.

I didn't know what to tell him. Lucille was a potter, and met Ethan at a trade show at the convention center the year before. He specialized in black and white photography of storm wreckage. Ethan seemed to have a thing for damaged trees. Trees split in half. Trees surrounded by water or other burnt trees. And trees that appeared to spring from destroyed homes. Lucille thought his work was an elegant representation of resilience. I didn't see anything in the pictures except desolate trees in shitty landscapes.

"I don't know, man. I didn't see it coming. I mean I knew she liked his work and they kept in touch. But I thought they were just friends." I sipped my beer.

I didn't tell Devin that I knew this was bullshit. Lucille saw Ethan every chance she could. She attended any out of town trade show where he hawked his tree portraits. And she made sure these trips occurred when I was too busy to go with her. Finally last month, I came back to our apartment to find she'd moved out, leaving a note that simply read: *I'm moving to Oklahoma with Ethan.* No excuse or explanation, no fuck you, just that she was moving.

"Good riddance, I say." Devin popped an olive in his mouth and kept an eye out for the band. The waitress brought us each another beer. I split my attention between the crowded room and the street outside. And I indulged in my newly acquired nervous habit of rubbing my hair. I started at the back of my neck, then worked my way up to the crown.

Devin snapped his fingers. "Take it easy. You're gonna rub yourself bald."

I slowly withdrew my hand and placed it on the table. I tried to smile at Devin, but couldn't tell if my muscles ever accomplished the task.

"How you holding up?"

I bit my lip. "It's funny the things you discover you miss. Like the sounds of someone in bed next to you."

"If all you want is a woman to snore in your bed, hell, this city's got a whole district of strip clubs." He took a quick pull from his beer. "We can go there next."

I examined Devin's face. His brow and eyes were already crisscrossed with lines. *One for each girl,* he would proudly declare. His cheeks were clear, not pimpled like in the old days. The brown hair was buzzed close to his skull now, favoring simplicity and efficiency of care over style when he started working more and performing less. He hardly resembled the guy who used to play forklift chicken with me in the warehouse. The one who had the brilliant idea, stoned and drunk on his ass, of asking a pizzeria to deliver us back to our apartment, rather than get a cab. Only his slanted, cocky smirk hadn't changed.

When I didn't react to his suggestion, Devin dropped the strip clubs and made small talk about his current girlfriend. Andrea was a beekeeper, with sixty hives in Battle Ground. Apparently one of the hives had become infected with a parasite. Some kind of fly, he couldn't remember exactly, laid their eggs inside the bees. The larvae ate the bees from the inside. As the bees were gutted, their behavior changed in bizarre ways. They flew around at night, attracted to bright lights like moths, ultimately devolving into what Devin described as zombie bees.

Devin grew more animated as the beer kicked in and he warmed to the idea of zombie insects. "In the end, they just fly around mindlessly looking for light, for life. Probably want to crawl in somebody's ear and sting'em in the brain." He shuddered. "I wish Andrea didn't raise bees. They're the pricks of the insect world, always running into you and getting pissed." He finished his glass. "If anyone should be pissed, it should be me."

I nodded. Took another sip of my beer and wondered if Devin noticed the slight tremor in my hand.

"When you coming back to work?"

I knew the question was coming, but still had no answer. I opened my mouth, and stuttered, making several false starts at a reply, but nothing came. Before I could collect myself, the band took the stage and the noise diverted Devin's attention.

The already dim lights in the room were lowered. Spots illuminated the stage, directing the attention of the audience to the band. I watched Devin's head bob with the beat. Gradually the music washed over me and I was forced to relax a little. But then someone would light a cigarette and whatever power the music held would pass.

With each strike of a match or click of a lighter, I felt my shoulders tense, and my heart compress in my chest. I watched as other members of the audience took long drags on their cigarettes. In the darkened room the glowing red butts were evil eyes staring, accusing me.

I shaved my depression beard to hide the evidence of my actual suicide attempt the week before. I'd turned on the gas stove, looking for the easy way out. My plan was to lean back at the kitchen table, doze off and not wake up. Slowly, the room developed that unpleasant propane smell, that unnatural odor added to warn of impending danger. My folded hands began to rattle against the kitchen table. And so I developed the brilliant idea to calm myself with one last smoke. The resulting fireball knocked my ass to the floor, and singed my beard and eyebrows. The shock had quenched my thirst for death. I turned off the stove, opened the windows and retreated back to bed.

A woman joined the band on stage. She sat poised at the baby grand piano in a thin-strapped burgundy dress. Her black hair framed a round face. Devin wanted to know what I thought of her. She was pretty, but reminded me too much of pictures I'd seen of my grandmother when she was young. I told Devin she wasn't my type. He shrugged and returned his slack-jawed stare to her eyes, shimmering beneath the spotlights.

She led the band in a rendition of "In My Life," which seemed an odd choice for a jazz club. Her version was slower and more soulful than the Beatles. I caught myself wondering if Lucille would have liked it. The woman's voice was probably too stripped down for her. I'd always thought the true test of a musician's worth was how they sounded live. This woman's voice was clean, without the over-produced, showy quality of most contemporary singers. The types of singers Lucille downloaded singles from. Her presentation was quiet, relying on her emphasis on certain lyrics to underscore the somber nature of the ballad. She sang with her eyes closed.

While Devin continued to ogle the singer, a different woman caught my eye. I studied the waitress, her blonde hair pulled into a ponytail, thick-rimmed glasses too large for her delicate face, framing her blue eyes. She wore black slacks with a black polo shirt. The Fremont Bridge was tattooed in blue ink on her left bicep, and gave the illusion that one arm was larger than the other. Bulbous even. As though she had exclusively weight trained on one side of her body.

I watched as the waitress danced through the narrow alleys between tables. She was a pro, always in time with the music, never blocking the customers, sure of herself even when weighed down with trays. I savored the way her polo rode up as she delivered drinks, drank in the pale strip of her exposed lower back. I longed for a connection, for her to notice me. But more than anything, I wanted to place my hand on the small of her back.

I tapped Devin on the shoulder and signaled, with my hand tipping toward my mouth, that I was going to the bar for a drink. He nodded and held up two fingers. I waded through the tables until the waitress stood directly in my path, her back to me. "Excuse me," I said. My hand hovered over the small of her back, but I didn't dare touch her as I waited to pass. She turned and smiled, her blue eyes magnified by her glasses. We awkwardly maneuvered in the tight space, until I was in the clear on the other side.

At the bar I ordered a shot of whiskey and two more Hefeweizen. On stage, the alto sax player stood for his solo. The waitress continued to make her rounds, our encounter just a blip in her evening's work. I suspected she was a student in her mid-twenties, dreaming of moving on and getting out. Just like Devin and I did whenever we took the stage, our current girlfriends hawking our CDs in a dark corner booth. As I downed the shot, I wondered if there were any jukeboxes in Portland that still had Animatronic Cowboy's demo. The whiskey burned as it ran down my throat. My stomach was sour and I already dreaded the morning hangover.

The piano chords coated the ridges and recesses of my mind as I lingered at the bar and watched the scene in the bar's huge mirror. Outside, people shuffled down the street, drawn along the pavement by the neon signs, just as I had been. Couples looking for a quiet spot, young men looking to get laid, and young women out on the pretense that they just wanted to dance. Reasons to drink used to slide effortlessly from my tongue, but now those words seemed foreign to me. It was a language that Devin, Lucille and Ethan were still fluent in. But somewhere along the way, I had lost my ear.

The waitress set her tray next to me on the bar. She didn't sit but leaned back, propped up by her elbows. I watched her shoulders rise and fall in the mirror. "You know there's a series of tunnels under this part of town," I said, not turning to face her. "Run out to the river."

She turned and gave me the same smile she had among the tables. "Yeah, the owner uses one as a storeroom. Want to see?"

I smiled, gestured at the beers and cocked my head back toward the table. "Just let me take these to my friend."

The song finished, the siren stood and bowed. Devin whistled and stomped his foot, shaking the table. The set was over; there would be a thirty-minute intermission. He took his beer and caught the alto sax player on his way to the bar. Devin complimented him on his playing but really wanted to know more about the singer.

I rose to leave, to meet the waitress, to escape the light and to breath in the darkness. Beneath my jacket, I noticed my shirt clung to my body with sweat. Devin reached out and grabbed my arm as I passed: "Where you going, man? The band really cuts loose during the second set. Starts experimenting."

I thought of the way Lucille would have crinkled her nose at this, and made some snotty comment about how inaccessible jazz was, and I was tempted to stay. But I couldn't keep making decisions because of her.

"Nah, I got to get up for work tomorrow."

Devin let go of my arm and nodded. "See you there."

In the basement, amongst the crates of liquor, the waitress leaned forward next to an old jukebox, half covered with a drop cloth. She was partially concealed by shadow. I wondered if the jukebox had our demo inside. She watched as I moved the cases of wine that concealed the entrance to the tunnel. Directly overhead was the frame of a trap door. Chains and shackles hung from the brick archways, and a pile of leather shoes was discarded just behind the crates. This darkness once swallowed men who couldn't hold their liquor, and naïve women who didn't watch their drinks.

The waitress placed her hand on my shoulder. I turned away from the Shanghai tunnel, the chains, and the shoes. Faced her and the club's storage room, lit by one naked bulb overhead. "Nothing in there for you," she said. "Just mold and ghosts." She leaned in and I kissed her, my hand placed on the small of her back.

After the kiss I turned back toward the tunnel. I felt her breath on my cheek, sweet, not like the sour breath of the tunnel. "Break's over," she said. "I've got to get back up. You staying for the second set?"

I shook my head. "Gotta work tomorrow."

We exchanged information. Promised to call. She stood at the bottom of the stairs. I didn't move, still transfixed by the dark, blank corridor that opened before me. "Can I trust you to slip out without being seen?" she finally said.

I nodded, not at her but at the tunnel's arched entrance. She disappeared up the stairs. I stood for a moment longer but the darkness had changed. Perhaps it was the openness, seeing the tunnel exposed without the boards. Or that the smell was different, mixed with the waitress' sweet breath.

Still, I couldn't take my eyes off the black hollow as I slowly backed my way toward the stairs.

Upstairs the band had started their second set. Devin had taken my place on the bench that ran along the window. His arm draped above the bare shoulders of the singer. I looked at Devin and saw a person that knew how to begin again, at least when it came to women. I needed to begin again. Or perhaps more precisely, I needed to resume. Flex my hand. Tune the guitar. Rent some studio time. Even if the end result didn't matter, that didn't cheapen the importance of the effort.

The waitress continued her dance among the tables. Her movement was more sporadic than before, matching the more improvised tunes. I double-checked that her number was still in my pocket and made my way to the door.

The air outside was cold, a welcome change from the warm, smoke-filled club. I lowered my eyes and ignored the neon signs. Instead, I followed the cracks in the sidewalks. Every now and then, a grate allowed the darkness to seep up from Portland's underground. I let the chilled air and the old sidewalks lead me to the Galleria station, to wait for the Blue Line.

Community Service

The name on everyone's lips at Camas High School that Tuesday was Tonya Harding. The infamous figure skater had been sentenced for assaulting her boyfriend back in February. Darren had forgiven her for punching his face into a bruised and bloody patchwork, and throwing a hubcap at his head. But despite his pleas for leniency, the judge had ordered a weekend in jail and ten days of community service. Her first day on the work crew would bring her to the Camas Cemetery, just a few blocks from the school. And word spread quickly.

This was before Harding's public rehabilitation. Before she would attempt to parley the publicity into a boxing career. Before she competed on *Dancing with the Stars,* or got the Hollywood treatment with a biopic starring an Australian starlet. Back then, she was just a figure skating instructor at a Portland mall. Until her arrest most people had forgotten Tonya Harding still lived in southwest Washington. Carly certainly had. Carly didn't care about Tonya Harding, but she was all her best friend Nicole could talk about.

"She's a total badass," Nicole said. "I can't believe she lives in our town."

"You still coming over Friday to study?"

They took their seats at a vacant table near the corner of the cafeteria. Carly deliberately selected the table out of the natural view of the junior girls. Nicole had been hanging out with them since their math instructor implemented an assigned seating chart. They'd invited Nicole to a party Friday night. Carly was not on the guestlist. When Nicole wasn't talking about Tonya Harding, she was talking about the junior girls. Both topics had quickly grown tedious to Carly.

"Can't. Got to get ready for the party." Nicole smiled. "To make a good impression for both of us."

Carly and Nicole had been best friends since they were in the same second grade class at Lacamas Heights Elementary. Initially, they bonded over the shared social inadequacy of parents unwilling to buy them *American Girl* dolls. Nicole quickly overcame this status signaling snag by projecting the biggest personality in the room. No matter the situation, she had an anecdote, joke or smart comment. This was not a sustainable option for the introverted Carly, who relied on her friend for inclusion. For most of their friendship, Nicole had to convince other kids to include Carly in their activities. Carly was painfully aware of her status as an appeasement. She'd overheard the other girls complain that the only reason she'd been invited to a middle school sleepover was because Nicole insisted. "She may be your friend, but that doesn't mean we have to like her," one of the girls hissed in a hushed tone when Carly left the room to brush her teeth. She'd waited around the corner for them to switch topics before re-entering. This allowed everyone to pretend the incident had never occurred.

Usually, they spent their afternoons together. Nicole was a fixture at Carly's house after school. Doing homework, listening to music as Nicole dished the latest gossip and they planned their future summers in Europe or Japan, and practicing soccer. But since the junior girls' interest, she'd been less available, more distant, at least within the confines of school. The friends still hung out and studied together, just not where anyone of teenage social distinction could witness their interactions. When she did grace Carly with her presence, Nicole became more critical of her. With an affected tone, she would tell Carly that people would like her more if she spent less time studying and updated her clothes. Carly would silently argue the guys didn't seem to mind attempting to sneak a peek down her overalls every chance they got, even though her tops were baggier than the tight stuff the other girls wore. She knew, however, that Nicole would deny this new dynamic to their friendship, so there was little reason to challenge the extra judgement.

All she could hope was that the junior girls would grow bored with Nicole, and she'd get her friend back. But as their conversations became more focused on the junior girls and Tonya Harding, and they saw less and less of each other, Carly couldn't help but feel Nicole was pulling away. Worse, she began to wonder if Nicole was ashamed of her.

"It's only temporary," she said. "Until I'm established. Then of course I'll introduce you. Insist even. You've got nothing to worry about. I'll call you Saturday after the party, promise."

"I understand." Carly kept her eyes locked on the center of the table.

"I wish you'd reconsider letting them look at your homework." Nicole rotated her Snapple bottle between her palms. "It's what friends in a study group do. It'd probably get you invited to the party. What's it really going to hurt?"

"It's cheating."

"Whatever." Nicole scooped her uneaten lunch back into her brown paper bag and tossed it in the trash. Across the cafeteria, one the junior girls spotted Nicole and gestured for her to come over. "We're going to see Tonya. I'd ask you to join, but it's against the rules for sophomores to leave campus."

Carly watched as Nicole crossed the cafeteria and stood at the upper-class table. She'd adopted their annoying habit of speaking not just with her hands but her whole arms. Nicole flailed like a baseball manager who'd forgotten his team's signs. Everything about the interaction, Carly knew, was exaggerated for show. Her friend wanted to make sure everyone saw who she was with. Recognition would cement her new status. The group rose from the table in unison and headed for the exterior doors.

Carly sat alone at the table. The room buzzed with students. She watched Nicole, surrounded by the older girls, walk straight out of the cafeteria. Her friend did not look back as they headed toward the cemetery. Carly wanted to scream, to run to the first staff member she could find and turn Nicole in. Let her sit alone in the office, she thought. Dalton eased into the chair next to Carly. She couldn't say she was happy to see him, although she was glad not to be seen sitting totally alone. He leaned back in his chair, head tilted toward the high ceiling as though he were counting the pock marks in the tiles.

"How's it going Goat Girl?" He brought the front legs of his chair down with an emphatic clap.

Dalton had dubbed Carly with this nickname in second grade when he'd found out she raised goats. He even attempted to convince their class that she smelled like one. To her relief, despite his fanatical devotion to the moniker, it had never caught on.

"What do you want, Dalton?"

He rummaged through his backpack and produced his red hunting hat. He jammed the wool hat, too warm for May, down on Carly's head. Her brown curly hair stuck out in uneven clumps at the fabric's edges like grass along a neglected fence line. "Think we passed our presentation?"

Their English teacher had assigned them a presentation together on *The Catcher in The Rye*. It was one of the few classes Carly didn't have in common with Nicole. The teacher had saddled her with Dalton, the only other student without a willing partner. They'd planned for him to focus on the connotative meaning behind Holden Caulfield's question "Where do the ducks go when the pond freezes over?"

But Dalton had wandered in just before the end of class, leaving her to stammer through most of the speech alone. He was there just long enough to slap a red hunting cap on backwards, waggle his finger across the class, including their teacher, and declare "You're a bunch of phonies," to uproarious laughter as the bell rang. He stole the show, for their classmates at least.

Carly could only hope that their teacher had paid more attention to her carefully constructed points than his antics. The "pond" represented circumstances in a person's natural environment. J. D. Salinger wanted his readers to consider what they would do when faced with uncertainty. Holden's concern for the ducks in the Central Park lagoon revealed his fear of change. If the pond was lost, did the duck start acting like another animal? How could a person move on when everything she knew was lost? Did she abandon her plans when things started going wrong? Holden was unable to imagine the ducks adapting, and found himself unsettled at the notion of altering his life to survive. Holden, Carly explained to the class, was a human duck, struggling to find himself in a new habitat.

Carly wondered what Nicole's obsession with Tonya Harding revealed about her struggle.

"No thanks to you," she said. "But I think I did enough for both of us."

He shrugged.

"You're welcome," she said. "Why were you late, anyway?"

"Lot of little things, really. Slept through my alarm. Woke up late. Missed the bus. Oh, and all my socks were in the wash." He slapped his red Puma sneakers on the table. "Had to wear a moist pair straight from the dryer."

"Don't use that word," she said. "It's disgusting."

"What word?"

"Moist." She pulled the hat from her head and flung it on the table.

"Relax, it's just a word. There's nothing inherently disgusting about it. Whatever hang-ups you've got about it are entirely your own."

"No, trust me, it's a word to be avoided. Especially when you're talking to women."

"How do you describe cake, then? *It's so damp and delicious,*" he said in a falsetto. "Sounds so much better." Dalton grabbed the hat from the table. He started to stuff it back in his bag, but then put it on instead.

"Whatever, you're a pervert."

He shrugged. "Suit yourself, Goat Girl. Where's Nicole?"

"Gawking at Tonya Harding with her new friends."

"Can't say I understand the appeal." He leaned back and stretched, daring one of the lunchroom aides to tell him to take the hat off in the building. "Hey, remember pogs? I've got a Tonya Harding slammer from elementary school. It's one of the heavier ones, meant to flip the cheap cardboard ones you were supposed to play with, as if anyone did anything other than collect 'em. It's got an outline of a leg bent at the knee etched in shiny, faux-metallic purple lines. A hand clutching a bat hovers above the kneecap, with jagged lines to indicate motion, force and collision. Below the knee it reads *Why me?* And *TONYA SLAMMER* wraps around the edge, just above the bat. Think I could sell it now that she's infamous again?"

"Stop talking."

"Sheesh, what's gotten into you?"

Carly sighed and looked at the seat normally occupied by Nicole.

"That's it?" he said. "Then just go gawk at Tonya Harding yourself."

She started to object, but could think of no real reason she shouldn't take Dalton's advice and show Nicole she wasn't socially hopeless. Still she hesitated. "Will you go with me?"

Dalton smiled. "Sure, why not."

Carly matched Dalton's confident, non-flinching stride through the hallway. She wished he'd ditched his hunting hat. To her the red and black flannel constituted an unnecessary risk.

"The key is looking like you don't know you're doing anything wrong," he whispered. "That way you plead ignorance and ask for forgiveness if you get caught."

She felt utterly exposed without the cloak of upper-class girls that Nicole utilized. They slipped out of the building into the late May sun. She felt her heart rate escalate and rise into her tightening throat with each step across the student parking lot. Carly was positive she hadn't breathed until they were safely across the street and out of sight near the practice soccer field.

They took an unassuming place away from the others peering through the junipers that masked the perimeter of the cemetery. Carly and Dalton took shelter beneath the wide shadow the Doc Harris stadium scoreboard cast over the first stretch of graves and the single lane road that separated these elite markers from the rest of the cemetery. The other gawkers clustered like a swarm of bees searching for a spot to establish a new hive after the colony split. At first, Carly couldn't see Tonya Harding among the orange vested work crew and armed guards. Then she emerged.

Tonya Harding walked between the headstones, slightly hunched by the weight of the gas powered weedwhacker slung over her shoulder with a black strap. Her blonde hair was pulled back into a ponytail with a scrunchy and a pair of aviator sunglasses glinted below her bangs. She wore a plain white t-shirt tucked into a pair of jeans and an orange safety vest. The sunglasses made it difficult to tell how much attention she paid to the gathering crowd. A mix of reporters, neighborhood busybodies, and giggling students on lunch break. But there could be little doubt they were all there for her.

But why were they all there, Carly wondered. To see Tonya Harding strike a guard? Abuse a reporter? Attempt an escape? Did any of them really expect her do anything other than mow the grass, weed flower beds and roughly edge the flat stones with the weedwhacker? Carly realized that for most of the onlookers, the answer was simple. They wanted to feel a part of something larger than themselves. Seeing a celebrity, even a diminished star like Tonya

Harding, in the real world made their own lives seem just a bit more special. They'd all be able to talk about the day they saw the Olympic figure skater at their local cemetery.

While this scene was more perverse, it struck Carly that it wasn't any different than when Dad recounted the time they'd seen Ken Griffey Jr. having dinner with his family at the Planet Hollywood in Seattle. His favorite part of the story was how he'd wished the Kid good luck as he left the restaurant carrying his young son in route to the ballpark. That alone made the overpriced hamburgers worthwhile to Dad. And she could picture him retelling it, for the thousandth time, when Junior got inducted into Cooperstown.

It was the same reason he'd taken Carly to school late one chilly fall morning after watching the Olympic torch run through Portland. And she had to confess that she'd felt special, waltzing into her elementary school classroom with only a few minutes left before first recess. She'd relished the jealous look on Nicole's face when she'd explained her tardiness to the teacher in a mock bashful tone, though still loud enough for the whole class to hear. Everyone in class wanted to talk to Carly that day, and for once it had nothing to do with Nicole.

Slowly the crowd thinned out. The reporters had their shots and all the comments they would receive from the supervising officers. Nothing more appeared likely to happen. After all, in the end it was just a work crew. They'd finish cleaning the cemetery, put away their gear, and either be transported to another site or released after returning to the rendezvous point. The officers looked relieved as more people drifted away. No doubt they hoped everyone's morbid curiosity had been satisfied. If Tonya Harding continued to turn work crew into a sideshow, they'd have to figure out some other way for her to complete her community service.

Dalton looked at his watch. "Seen enough, Goat Girl?"

"For now," Carly said. As they joined the stream of students headed toward campus, she spied Nicole and the junior girls. They would be buzzing in math class that afternoon, especially Nicole. As far she knew, she was the only underclassmen to see Tonya Harding that afternoon. Carly imagined how dejected her friend would be when she realized they'd treaded on her privilege. Her friend probably wouldn't speak to her for at least a week, as punishment for stealing this moment.

Dalton worked his way up the crowd, steadily gaining on Nicole. Carly hooked his elbow and settled his pace. They merged into the middle-back of the throng of students as they converged on the building. A pair of anonymous faces in the crowd that veered off away from Nicole's locker. With his elbow, Carly steered both of them around the gym to approach the sophomore lockers from the cafeteria. To her surprise, Dalton didn't resist. Nor did he say a word about Tonya Harding to Nicole or anyone else. He instinctively withdrew his arm, as they rounded the corner and Nicole, primping at her locker, came into view.

California Sunshine

The day finally arrived when Gil would take Elise to the Spokane Greyhound station. He didn't know exactly when she had resolved to leave, although he should have seen it coming. But Elise was making her escape today, leaving him to monitor the European Gazelle beetle invasion alone.

She was leaving that afternoon. He'd helped pack her bags the night before. They sat in the living room, Elise chattering away, folding her clothes, tightly cramming every inch of available space in her two suitcases. It seemed strange to him that their clothes would never comingle in the wash again. Gil wondered if he would ever intimately know someone else's sock and underwear drawer, the way he knew Elise's. Did she have any thoughts like this, any doubts? Probably not, she made the whole thing look easy.

A garbage bag of useless things sat next to the front door, waiting for Gil to take them to Value Village. Heavy sweaters, woolen socks, and winter clothes, things Elise wouldn't need in California. That morning, she packed her toiletries in the bathroom, whistling as she removed the last traces of herself from their apartment. But for Gil, it felt like she'd left months ago.

When they first met, Elise would lay his head in her lap and read him poetry from books with bright covers that she picked up at the library on her way home from work. The selections were standard public school fare: Shakespeare's sonnets, Walt Whitman, Langston Hughes and Dylan

Thomas. She thought he looked like Thomas. He loved the way she softly enunciated every word and stroked his hair; the gentle rhythm of her speech often lulled him to sleep. Gil didn't understand poetry or why Elise enjoyed it. The difference between a good poem, signaled by crinkling her nose, and a bad poem, signaled by pulling her mouth to one side, remained an enigma. But he loved the way she read, her special cadence and flow.

He couldn't remember when she stopped reading to him. It was probably after the first winter, when she'd reminded him that California remained her destination. She was reading Gary Snyder. *Another California transplant,* she told him.

She was originally from Omaha and Gil knew that she always dreamed of the west. Spokane was simply a waystation, as far as her savings took her on the bus. Elise never intended to stay. She was pulled on by the illusion of choices in California. But then the first winter passed and the snow melted, and she stopped talking about leaving. Gil assumed their life together had replaced those dreams.

She suggested he join her. After all, like Elise, Gil never intended to end up in Spokane. He'd followed work east after graduating from high school, picking fruit and sleeping in his car. Still Gil remained noncommittal and unenthusiastic toward the invitation. He'd already relocated once, from the westside of the Cascades and had little desire to uproot himself to a more remote location, just to live near some palm trees. Gradually, she stopped asking, became a distant presence. She haunted the apartment, felt but not seen or heard. She stopped going to work and hunkered down next to the sputtering air conditioner, reading to herself. Finally, he suggested she go ahead to get settled, without him.

He probably should have thanked her for the distance. It would make things easier when she finally left. He'd already grown used to her absence. That morning, all Gil could do was sit and watch her pack, admiring the apparition confined between those walls for the last time.

He didn't think it was hard for Elise to leave him behind. And why not, she was getting what she wanted. On that last day, it didn't seem she could get out fast enough. She double-checked every pantry and drawer in the place. Elise had kept trinkets, little figurines and maps in every room of their apartment. Gil supposed she wanted to make sure everything was taken care of, because she didn't think he would know what to do if he suddenly discovered that she'd left her deodorant. He was amazed she trusted him to drop that bag of unwanted clothes off at Value Village.

They didn't talk, she provided all the narration. She hovered, while he watched, the only audience member at an over-rehearsed magic show: *Watch as I make myself disappear*. Her imminent departure suddenly bothered Gil more than he realized. With a few hours before her bus, he decided to go check one of his traps rather than sit there, feeling stuck in the middle.

As a seasonal employee for Spokane County, Gil monitored all insect traps scattered around a 20-mile radius of the city. He actually discovered the first beetle, out on the highway median in mid-May. Its bulbous black body was stuck to the adhesive, legs futilely kicking in the air. Elise was with him; she'd crinkled her nose and muttered *poor thing* as he fumbled with his laminated identification cards. He scoured the images, but none were quite right.

Initially, his inability to identify *Nebria brevicollis* worried Gil. He'd only been on the job for a few weeks. The chief entomologist might scoff at his incompetence, even terminate him. But far from a reprimand, his discovery was met first with skepticism, then with excitement. An article in the local paper quoted him about his find, and he was asked to lead several special training sessions. Tracking the celebrity beetle became the agency's highest priority that summer.

Elise reveled in his brief quasi-celebrity. He heard her on the phone telling friends and family how other lazy bug trappers would have just identified the EGB as the closest species without a second thought, but not him. Gil didn't understand the obsession with the EGB. He seldom found them in his traps and they looked almost identical to other, more common bugs. The effects of their sudden presence were still unknown. So far, the beetle wasn't the scourge of anything that people cared about. No commercial crops were being devoured, no precious trees killed. The EGB could run down and kill any other invertebrate it came across, but the victimized insects weren't exactly the farmer's friends. The new invasive species was a priority mainly as a curiosity. Still, Gil wondered, if the public's interest hadn't waned, if he'd just found a few more EGBs, would Elise still be leaving?

Gil figured he'd walk down, log the species and deaths, change the adhesive strips if needed, and be back in plenty of time. His absence would give her the opportunity to celebrate openly before boarding the bus to Salinas. But as he grabbed his county issued satchel, filled with logbooks and trap supplies, and headed for the door, she paused halfway between the living room and their bedroom.

"Where are you going?" Her voice was thin.

"Out to check the trap in the sunken neighborhood.

Don't worry, I'll be back in time to take you to the station."

She studied him. Really looked at Gil for the first time in months. Probably suspected that he was trying to ruin her plan with tardiness. "Can't the bugs wait a day?"

"If I don't check that one every few days, the strips get crowded." It was a lie. But he needed to get out of the apartment, away from her triumphant packing. Gil needed to clear his head before the ride to the station. She could erase the past two years without a witness. If she didn't care, he didn't want to care either.

"Hold on." She finished wrapping a ceramic kitten he had mistakenly bought her at a flea market for her birthday last year. Elise placed the bundle on top of her purse, walked over to the door and stepped into her flip-flops. "I'm coming too."

He shrugged and followed her out the door. Although it was still early, outside a heavy heat had already descended upon the streets. Gil and Elise crossed Riverside Drive and made their way toward the staircase to the Peaceful Valley, an area they called the sunken neighborhood. The street was quiet, as most people had already made their way to work. An occasional car sputtered by. A few joggers and dog walkers dodged the couple, hugging the edge of the sidewalk, taking advantage of the shade provided by the oaks and maples that lined the street.

Gil knew that Elise was escaping. California was all she seemed to talk about since the first snows of December. She dreamed aloud about sunshine and sandy beaches. Lights, money, and glamorous, laidback people. The Golden Coast. She ignored his remarks about crime rates, traffic jams, smog and the high cost of living.

The idea started as a rhetorical question one morning when he drove her to work. *Wouldn't it be nice to live somewhere where it didn't matter that the heater in the car was broken?* They were waiting for a light, both heavily bundled against the cold. He had agreed that it would make things easier. As the snow failed to melt, her purpose became clearer, and the questions turned to statements.

But she didn't talk about him going anymore. Now when she spoke of exploring shimmering cities, built on cliffs that overlooked the ocean, with never a day below 60 degrees, she was alone. Gil first noticed the change in the narrative from *We* to *I* at the beginning of summer. A conceit built around the false compromise that he would join her in the fall, once his contract expired and she had things settled. For the sake of harmony, he didn't comment on the semantic shift.

For most of her stay in Spokane, Elise had worked at a diner near Gonzaga. One of those places that stayed open 24 hours a day and never stopped serving breakfast. Gil appreciated this policy and the leftover pancakes she occasionally brought him. He insisted that breakfast was a meal, not a time of day. He had met her there two summers ago. She was only two weeks off the bus from Omaha. He watched her from across the diner, but couldn't look her in the eye whenever she came to his table.

Gil was surprised when Elise decided to accompany him to the trap before her bus departed. As they walked, he scanned the sidewalk, trying to think of something to say. He didn't want to question her renewed interest; pressing might change her mind. Because of the heat, he had only planned on checking one site that day, the site closest to their apartment. The trap was placed in the scrubby pine and sagebrush of the gravel strips along the river. Most of the city was situated on basalt bluffs, overlooking the shallow river. Below the southern cliffs, a narrow shelf of shore served as a buffer between the canyon wall and the river. A curious hodgepodge had sprouted on this shelf. Although proximity to the river would seem to be a desirable location, flooding had delayed settlement and development. The result was a strange mixture of new luxury homes crowned with solar panels next to rundown cottages with moss-covered roofs.

Gil and Elise descended the graffiti-covered staircase three blocks from their apartment down onto the flats. Their own apartment was in Browne's Addition, the oldest part of Spokane, and sat on the ridge overlooking the sunken neighborhood. Their basement unit's high windows granted them a sliver of fire safety and a view of shoes on the sidewalk outside. The brick and mortar building mixed company with the gutted and divided Victorian homes that comprised its companions. The unit wasn't glamorous. But for Gil and Elise, transplants in Spokane, it served as home.

Elise paused before starting down. "The air is too stagnant and muggy. Just like in Omaha. Makes the heat almost unbearable," she said. "Carol says the sea breezes in Salinas act like a natural air conditioner."

"I suppose, but the salty air is awfully corrosive. You know how often people on the coast have to paint their houses?"

She turned away and continued to cut through the heavy air toward the bottom.

The slope by the stairs was scarred with remnants of past structures and hobo encampments. Dilapidated retaining walls, brick smoke stacks and shards of a parallel collapsed staircase rested with other human refuse on the hillside. Crooked pine trees stretched toward the sun, but their tops had been cut short to accommodate the crisscross of overhead power lines and the Maple Street Bridge. The whole area had the feel of a secret room, boarded off at the back of a forgotten cellar.

They paused on the first landing of the rusted staircase, halfway down the slope. The morning sun shone brightly over the beige landscape below. Overhead, cars rattled across the bridge. Its great cement legs pierced the center of a grass park near the river. The bridge shaded several houses, the park, and a basketball court. Gil wondered what it would be like to live directly beneath the bridge, with all natural light blocked or provided from cockeyed angles. The constant noise of cars overhead. He'd hate it.

"You know Carol's place down there, where I'll be staying, has a huge outdoor pool. An apartment complex with a pool, can you believe that?"

He could. There were plenty of buildings with communal pools around Spokane. He'd spent the summer they met skimming them, while she made fun of his hideous farmer's tan and complained that he reeked of chlorine. They had friends that lived in units with similar perks, and he couldn't recall her ever showing any interest in jumping in when the heat arrived. He wanted to ask her what made the pools in California so appealing, but thought better of it.

He reached down and took Elise's hand. They laced their fingers together to maximize skin contact, a physical sign he'd read once showed that they were still full of lust and longing for one another. Her fingers were cool against his, like the underside of a pillow. They walked down the remaining steps in silence, loosening and tightening their grip, as though they were communicating through some pressurized form of Morse code.

At night Gil traced the features of Elise's face. A practice she'd introduced that first summer after reading Raymond Carver's "Cathedral."

"I want to really see each other," she'd said.

Obscured by darkness, his fingers mapped her forehead, rose and fell with her slender nose, got tangled in her eyebrows. They detoured around her mouth and eyes before taking the long route down the edge of her jaw and back to her hairline. He imagined he could feel her freckles, that beauty mark near her ear. Gil attempted to commit her face to muscle memory. He became convinced his fingers could absorb her dreams through osmosis. His calluses gleaned information from her pores, discerning the grit and grime of some distant, unnamed city in southern California as the oils from their skin mixed together.

At the bottom they stepped onto the worn pavement. In the shade of the bluff and the bridge, a cool breeze provided relief from the heavy summer air. They stood in the shadows, damp with perspiration from the walk. Gil glanced at Elise, but her gaze was locked on the staircase as if she were thinking about the packing she still had to do. He wondered again why she'd come at all.

They stepped back into the bright sun. The neighborhood appeared washed out, dry and dusty, as if a coarse drop cloth splotched with dull greens and grays had been pulled over to conceal its homely organization. As it had for the past few months, any lustful messages telegraphed by their entwined fingers fizzled out in these simmering days. Elise released Gil's hand, and he led the way toward the riverbank.

The narrow streets slipped past cookie cutter houses with no lawns and vacant lots where only the foundations remained. One homeowner fenced his lawn in with skis. Another advertised a victory garden; the old wooden sign on a third marketed custom-made coffins. The sidewalks were cluttered with the hollow dried stalks of weeds, grown up through cracks in the cement.

Despite their apartment's position on the bluff, neither realized the sunken neighborhood existed until Gil accepted the bug-trapping job that spring. After placing his traps by the river for the first time, Gil had returned, eager to share his discovery. At first, she was curious about the Peaceful Valley. Now, it was just another shoddy district near where she used to live.

Although they had taken many walks through the sunken neighborhood that summer, at various times of day, they had never encountered anyone. There was tangible evidence of the existence of residents. Cars parked on different sections of the streets and driveways. Wisps of smoke rose from the houses on mornings in early spring. Yet the city buses and cars that drove down the only street into the area never seemed to stop or let anyone out. The cracked sidewalks were covered in chalk drawings and the lawns were littered with discarded toys, never in the same configuration. But the children were invisible to them. The only living things Gil and Elise encountered were old tomcats, fat red squirrels, and pairs of chortling magpies.

Gil spied the trap, dangling from the lower branches of an oak tree. He laid the trap on the ground near the exposed root tops. The trap had the appearance of a white paper lantern; it almost vanished when placed against the gray stones. Gil carefully opened the cover. The inside was lined with a sticky substance. Several moths and wasps still struggled in the clear glue, while others had already exhausted themselves, or torn their own bodies apart. It was a slow death that Gil didn't envy. He wondered why trapped insects didn't warn others to stay away.

Elise moved back toward the road. Since the discovery of the first EGB, she didn't like to see the product of Gil's labor. Although she teased him that she didn't want to be a witness at his murder trial, she seemed to actually be bothered by the cruel survey methods.

Gil pulled a small notebook from his pocket and began to tally and classify the victims. Every two weeks, he reported his findings back to the State office, which extrapolated the area's population based on his figures. Every few days he would return to each site to record the data, and change the death strips as needed. Gil knelt next to the trap, examining the bodies. When he was unsure of a species, he consulted pictures on several laminated sheets. The morning sun radiated off the stones and reddened his legs.

In the corner of his eye, he could see Elise's tan legs sway below her shorts. She stared back toward the street, as if she were examining some phantom car crash. On her last day in town, she tried a slightly different approach to the conversation they'd repeatedly commenced and abandoned over the last few months.

"Near San Diego, there's a bay where dolphins beach themselves. No one really knows why. It's as if something is drawing them to that strip of sand. Other dolphins migrate in and out of the bay just fine. It's just a few that get stuck."

He continued to examine the trap, double-checking the figures with narrowed eyes behind his sunglasses. Beads of sweat trickled down his face. He wiped his brow with the back of his hand and continued to count. No EGBs. When Gil failed to react, Elise continued.

"You aren't getting it." She leaned back on the heels of her thin flip-flops before bringing her toes back to rest on the gravel. "They don't know why the dolphins beach themselves. They're in perfect health. Obviously, they aren't meant to live on land. And they can't stay in the bay either. At first, they just released them back into the bay, figured they'll follow the others out to sea. But most of them wound up back on the beach. Almost like they're fixated on it. It's one particular beach. Carol told me about it."

Gil placed the strips of insects in a clear plastic bag and sealed the zip lock. He wrote the date and trap number on the bag in black marker. The sheets would be cross-examined to confirm his identifications and figures. As he stowed the body bag in his satchel, he noticed the kicking had stopped.

From his satchel he pulled a small glass vial of attractant. Gil liked to think of it as some insect sex hormone meant to blindly draw the beetles to his paper fortress. He pictured the little black shells swaggering up the tree, following the scent of cheap French perfume spritzed on a seductive exoskeleton. It smelled like rotten fruit to him. He replaced the strip and reassembled the trap.

As he hung the trap he responded to Elise, without looking at her. "Maybe they're trying to die. Captive dolphins commit suicide all the time."

She didn't seem to hear him, or to care about what he said. "Now, after they check the dolphins out, they release them away from the bay. It's like they can't find their own way out. The dolphins need to be guided to open waters."

"Sounds pretty pointless, if they don't even have sense enough to avoid the beach." He shouldered the bag and started to walk back to the weedy sidewalks. He listened for the crinkle of gravel behind him, to know that Elise was following.

"People have to constantly monitor that beach. A lot of people keep an eye out for lost dolphins, full crews of volunteers and scientists. It's how Carol met her fiancée, the lifeguard. She says he's gorgeous."

Gil paused as he reached the sidewalk and turned to face Elise. "But what does a lifeguard look like?"

"That's a silly question," she said. "They're people. Only they wear swimsuits to work. You've seen a lifeguard before."

He honestly couldn't recall ever seeing a lifeguard. There had been a community pool in his hometown, Camas, built in the 50s in Crown Park. High fences surrounded three cement basins, warmed only by the faint sun. Gil always thought the pool compound resembled a bunker. A silent sentinel at the top of a hill waiting, like the fallout shelter in the public library's basement, for a disaster that never came. But Gil had learned to swim in the frigid waters of the Washougal and Columbia Rivers. Bodies of water entered at his own risk.

During the off-season the pools were drained, and left to fill with fir needles from the trees that bordered the installation. One fall night, Gil had climbed the high fences. In the deep end of the main pool he'd found four mutinous tennis balls, launched from the neighboring courts, and an aluminum baseball bat. He stood on the cushion of needles, hidden from a full moon beneath the diving board, and balanced the bat in the palm of his hand. In the distance he could hear freight trains rattle past, following the Colombia River to the coast. None paused or gave the little mill town a second thought. That fall his father was sure he would get a promotion; instead the mill laid him off. That was the only time Gil had ever been in the city pool. And there was certainly no lifeguard on duty that night. He decided to let the subject go and turned back toward the stairwell.

Across the narrow street stood Gil's favorite house in the sunken neighborhood. A sky blue two-story town house with white trim. The gable was painted with a swirl of white puffy clouds, the type you always see in picture books. A warm color, on overcast days the house stood out, eclipsing the rest of the neighborhood. But on a clear day the house was nearly invisible, as the faux clouds blended in with the sky. The first time Gil brought Elise on his route, she couldn't see the house, even when he pointed it out to her. She kept looking at him strangely and wanted to know why he was so eager to show her a lot full of dandelions behind a rickety white picket fence.

That morning the only sign of the house was the flutter of brown striped curtains from the upstairs window and two white lawn chairs on the front porch that seemed to float above the lawn like clouds. He wondered why the owner hadn't used white curtains to add to the illusion. Gil debated whether the curtains were worth pointing out to Elise. Would she even be able to see them? Before he could decide, Elise was already half way down the block.

Back at the top of the stairs, they paused hot and panting. Gil watched as Elise sat on the rusted rail, feet and flip-flops dangling above the sidewalk. He leaned against a parking meter. Behind him, cars and bikes passed on their way downtown. Joggers and walkers cut between them, momentarily concealing Gil and Elise from one another.

"You've got Carol's address and my phone number won't change. Have to find a job first but I'll let you know as soon as I find a place of my own."

He nodded and moved across from Elise at the top of the staircase.

"I'll get things settled. You'll see by the time you come down in…when does your contract end?"

"Whenever the first frosts get here, probably October."

"So, a month and a half, two months tops. It won't be long."

"There might be more work, even after the trapping season is over. You know, I'm the regional Gazelle Beetle specialist for the moment."

"What could you tell them that isn't already in your reports?"

Gil didn't have an answer. Over his shoulder he heard voices. He couldn't discern what they said but the sound was definitely coming from the sunken neighborhood. Low, gravelly, men's voices. Gil turned to face Elise; if she heard the voices, she didn't react. He peered down the slope but couldn't see anything, just a washed out landscape and rooftops. Several pops, like a cap gun, echoed across the ravine and mixed with the voices. Then there was laughter, squealing children released to play. A thin thread of black smoke curled up toward the midday sun. Gil followed the smoke down to the particular backyard, but nothing moved. Still, he was satisfied that life had resumed in the Peaceful Valley in their absence.

He approached Elise. She was gazing off toward their apartment, feet still dangling. He placed his hands on either side of her face.

"What are you doing?" But she stayed still.

He placed a finger to her mouth. Gil removed her sunglasses then closed her eyes with the palm of his hand. She puckered her lips in anticipation of a kiss. Closing his own eyes he slowly took in her face with his fingers. Then he released her and stepped back, signaling it was all right for her to open her eyes again.

"What was that about?" Elise asked.

"Come on, let's get your bags," he said, turning toward their apartment. "You don't want to miss your bus."

Omega

Morgan anxiously waited for quitting time. While he struggled to break into Seattle's alt-folk music scene, he paid his bills at *Friend or Pho,* a SoDo Vietnamese sandwich and bubble tea shop. Linea had stopped in earlier, ordered her usual, then slipped him a note on the napkin as she paid; she'd be stopping by his place this evening.

Morgan and Linea had carried on this spy-drop correspondence for three years. She'd stop by the shop, order a black milk tea, then provide directions for their rendezvous concealed on a napkin. Her delicate handwriting slanted to the right corner in purple ink, concealed within the folds of the square fluffy paper. They never went out together and only saw each other socially in groups. The convenient cover for their relationship was school acquaintances and they knew many of the same people. But in their situation, appearances were everything.

Whenever possible she came out to see him play. Linea would lie to Terry, saying she was going to a movie or concert with her girlfriends. Morgan hated to listen to Linea describe these deceits. But he loved the way she leaned on the stage, a splash of bright color in his peripheral vision. And he loved the passion of their relationship, their secret love, nurtured in the back alleys of clubs, the back glances at parties, and his tiny apartment. He drummed on the counter with his fingers, eyeing the remaining customers, silently urging them to finish their plates and leave.

###

He'd known Linea since the fifth grade but only realized his affection for her in high school. Morgan had always been quick to love. He didn't idealize women, putting them on a pedestal, but he tried to treat them the way they should be treated. But the teenage girls he knew had a peculiar hankering for guys who handled them badly. Morgan's high school was a honeycomb filled with strong, intelligent, young women hanging on every word of some asshole. Without the killer instinct of an alpha male, Morgan found his interactions with the opposite sex bore little nectar.

Often, Morgan was banished to the friend zone, or ended up serving as the default guy. As Backup Boy, he would hold his tongue as his female friend cursed men after an over stimulated playboy cheated on her. Always in the back of his mind, he hoped that this phase would pass and that someday she would see him for what he was, and what they could be.

Morgan had a few quasi-relationships, always unofficial, always short, and always poorly ended. The girl would lead him around for months, even a year, drawing him in, and then pushing him away when he got too close or she received a better offer from a more prized male.

After one particularly brutal rejection by a future California starlet, Morgan was alone after an unproductive band practice, brooding over which sign he misinterpreted this time. Absent-mindedly strumming his nylon stringed parlor guitar, he stared up from the floor at the popcorn glaze on his ceiling. The phone rang, but he wasn't prepared to rehash tempo debates with the bass player. He sat at his desk to screen the call. Next to stacks of guitar tabs Morgan rediscovered the handmade card, a piece of blue tag board bent into a small folder, his name scrolled in boxy black capital letters across the front of a white square outlined in red. The inside contained the same excited letters, thanking him for his help on an essay, and wishing he'd be well soon. The card was signed with a heart from Linea; beneath her name she drew a little snail.

She'd always been a sweet and considerate girl. Involved with various volunteer projects. But she'd rather bullshit her way through free study hour with him than attend 6th grade symphonic band rehearsal. She looked great in a pair of volleyball spandex. And pestered him about learning yoga with her or wondered why he didn't enroll in honors classes.

Then Morgan realized that Linea was the only person who seemed to genuinely care about him at school. Since he'd known her, she always tried to include him, wanted to know if he was going to the football game Friday, or if he'd be at a party. Several times, she'd brought him batches of cookies, her latest gluten free experiment, for no discernible reason. While his other friends made up strange stories about why he was absent, she made him a card. And from this little seed of kindness she casually planted, love sprouted. He knew he wasn't the first guy to be attracted to her, and he definitely wouldn't be the last.

Her stain on his adolescent psyche did not fade with the progression of time. In school they remained just friends, running in similar circles and on paths that would periodically diverge and converge. Linea was never without a regular boyfriend. So, even though he longed to, Morgan never felt there was a good time to tell her how he felt. After graduation, she left their sleepy southwestern Washington town for a private college in Seattle. Morgan stayed close to home, playing with his band Animatronic Cowboy for the hipsters in Portland taverns at night, while serving coffee at Powell's for cash.

Quitting time finally came and Morgan rushed through closing. He put the chairs up on the tables, sticky vinyl on gummy dull glossed wood. Then swept and mopped the floor. Stray noodles, bits of bread, crumpled napkins, coins, flavor orbs, and other spills, both dry and wet, littered the restaurant. His orange sneakers squeaked across the moist surface. These tasks completed, Morgan hung his apron in the back. Everything in its place, the doors to the teashop locked, another shift done.

Morgan wasted no time. He headed directly to the bus stop, his worn out shoes padding softly on the sidewalks as he jogged down the block. When the timing was right, he had virtually no wait for the bus. But if closing took too long, it would be at least a half hour waiting in the damp, cool night. Tonight proved most efficient, and the bus pulled up just as Morgan arrived at the stop. He jumped on the sparsely populated bus and took a seat toward the middle. Morgan closed his eyes, resting, with a smile on his face; soon he would be back in Linea's arms.

After a couple years, Morgan believed that even his friendship with Linea had petered out. But two years as a near-townie proved enough for the troubadour. He fled the familiar banks of the Columbia River to seek his fortune on the shores of Puget Sound. This decision held unexpected consequences, as his path again converged with Linea.

Morgan and Linea reunited at a pretentious coffee shop on Mercer Island. He was performing an acoustic set with his new band, Janet Reno and the Somethings, at the café's open mike night. The band played five songs to a lukewarm response, as the crowd clanked their mugs and did their best to talk over them. Janet Reno and the Somethings finished their set, thanked them for the lackluster applause and plugged their next gig at a bar in the UDistrict that weekend. Off the tiny stage, carefully stowing his gear, Morgan suddenly confronted a familiar face.

"I knew it was you." Linea greeted him with a smile.

She looked different and the same all at once, but somehow more herself. Gone were the locks that hung just below her shoulders when curled, and at her mid-back when straightened. Instead her hair was cut short like Audrey Hepburn, if Hepburn had worn it tousled more than styled and listened to Ani DiFranco and Sex Pistols. Linea's rich blue eyes looked as big and bright as ever. She wore a satin olive dress that went to her mid thigh, dark stockings, and knee-high boots.

Morgan barely managed to stammer a greeting. She was as beautiful as he remembered. Suddenly, he felt self-conscious about his own disheveled appearance.

Morgan's hair was also shorter. Since graduation he'd ditched his straight shoulder-length blonde locks, opting for upturned strands that hung down to the nape of his neck. Unkempt sideburns shot down to his jaw, while stubble gave the rest of his face a dirty appearance. Admittedly, his couch surfing lifestyle didn't lend itself to the best hygiene. He looked like a Scandinavian herring fisherman: lean, pale, grungy and ready to head out to sea.

"How long've you been in town?"

Linea stared at him, apparently waiting for him to pick up the conversation. When he didn't, she moved it along herself: "Are you guys going on again tonight?"

"Ah, no."

"Want to grab a bite to eat or a cup of coffee?"

Morgan nodded his head like the village idiot.

"Great, just let me tell my friends I'm leaving, you know, so they won't worry."

While Linea said her goodbyes, Morgan finished packing his gear. Under his breath, he cursed his stupidity for getting tongue tied. After his disconcerted behavior, he was lucky she still wanted to hang out. Morgan knew that if he didn't calm down and get his act together, she would think he'd become some kind of sociopath. Now that she was back in his life, he had to play this just right.

Morgan entered his studio apartment on Capitol Hill. The sparsely furnished room somehow still had a crowded feel. The kitchen was cluttered with pans and dishes stacked on the counters and stove. Several potted plants lined the windowsill above the sink: Christmas cactus, spider plant, Venus flytrap, and a bonsai ficus Linea had given him as a house-warming present. The single main room was furnished with a dirty sleeper sofa that was rarely seen as a couch, a milk crate bedside table, cinderblock bookcases housing paperback novels and an old stereo, and a guitar amp. The rest of the space was taken up by disorganized crates of CDs, records, and tapes. The only things hanging on the wall were his laundry drying above the radiator, a Beatles poster, and his two guitars above the bed. The bathroom was a cramped broom closet with a toilet, shower and sink. The entire studio exuded a damp, moldy musk that Morgan tried to cover with incense and candles. Rather than remove the stench of mildew, the sweet vapors mingled and mixed with the pungent air, spawning unwieldy offspring. Unless someone desired that seedy motel look, Morgan's dank place was hardly the ideal location for a regular affair.

Since Linea moved in with her boyfriend two years prior, her cleaner more spacious place was no longer an option. Adulterers can't be choosers, so they focused on each other's company, and ignored the aroma and furnishings. Linea, an art history major in college, liked to affect the role of the free spirit. She claimed that she loved Morgan's dump of an apartment. The studio's raw bohemian quality fit her jaded, poetic lover perfectly. Morgan sometimes feared that if he ever became more than a poor singer-songwriter that she'd leave him, that the desperate nature of his life was the attraction.

Morgan forced the warped door of his apartment open, slipped his sneakers off at the entryway, and hung his keys and jacket by the door. Incense and candles were already battling the mildew to a draw, and a Beatles album, *Rubber Soul*, cracked away on the record player, letting him know he wasn't alone. Linea claimed a set of keys to his place when their tryst became a regular thing. For the sake of ritual, he dimmed the lights as he left the kitchen and entered the main room.

Linea stepped out of the closet bathroom, lit brilliantly from behind. A pale blue satin slip with cream lace trim clung to her thigh, partially concealing yellow underwear with the same trim. The slip accented her deep blue eyes, making them pop and shine like a calm lake in summer moonlight. She leaned in the doorway, one knee bent, her foot resting on the frame like a pin-up girl.

"New lingerie?"

"You noticed." Linea smiled and walked toward Morgan.

"How long do we have?" He took her in his arms and caressed the soft skin on the back of her neck.

"All night," she whispered. Linea slowly unbuttoned his kung-fu style work shirt, gently rubbing down his chest. She loosened and removed his belt. "Terry is visiting his parents this weekend. So, I thought we could play house. Do you like my new nightie?"

The muscles in Morgan's neck and lower back tensed at the mention of Terry. Morgan knew he was the other man, and didn't need to be reminded of it. In his mind, Linea's boyfriend was a subject best left unspoken.

"It's nice."

"Good." She played with his shaggy hair. "I got it with you in mind. You even get to see it first."

With that phrase, Morgan felt something inside him snap. He could no longer stand the little reminders and inequities that came with his status. The idea that seeing the lingerie first was an honor made him feel cheap. A sour taste, like spoiled *pho chua*, rose in the back of his mouth.

"We need to talk." He pulled her arms down from around his neck.

"About what?" She tried to close the gap between them and re-tangle their bodies.

Morgan dodged her, side stepping toward the window opposite his bed.

"I can't do this anymore," he said without looking at her.

"What're you saying, you don't find me attractive anymore, you don't love me?" She took a step toward him.

"No, it's not that at all. I just can't do this. I can't handle us anymore."

"You're breaking up with me?"

"How can I break up with you? We don't officially exist."

"This is about Terry."

"Don't say his name."

"Morgan, I love you. You know that." Linea stood directly behind him, and wrapped her arms around him. "What we've got is special. Don't throw it away."

Morgan turned around and looked deep into Linea's eyes. The blue pools around her pupils glistened with suppressed tears. Her sadness began to soften his rapidly hardening heart. All he wanted was to hold her, come home to her. But that couldn't happen as long as he was the bit on the side.

"How can you say you love me, and then go home to him? If you love me, leave him."

"It isn't that simple."

"Sure it is. If what we have is so special, leave him. Bye-bye Terry, good-fucking-riddance."

"That isn't fair, I can love you both."

"What isn't fair is letting me take care of you, and then going home to him. Telling me it is some kind of privilege to get to see your new underwear first. It isn't fair to me, the boyfriend of convenience, and it sure-as-hell isn't fair to him, the boyfriend of appearances. Are you ashamed to be with me?"

"No." She pushed away from him and moved toward the bed. Tears began to slowly run down her face. "It would be wonderful to be with you, freely, openly. I just can't choose." She slumped onto the edge of the mattress.

"You must've known someday you'd have to choose."

Morgan couldn't look at her anymore. He moved toward the kitchen and the door. He buttoned his shirt and slipped on his shoes.

"Morgan," she called as he reached the door, her voice cracked, as if it came from an overplayed record. "Are we over?"

He didn't answer. The door seemed heavier, the hinges turned stiffly. But somehow he managed to force it open, and himself into the hall. Behind him the door banged shut. And then for a moment there was silence. The tension of his single room slowly lifted in the stale air of the hall. Morgan stood there, staring at the cracked, water-damaged ceiling tiles.

###

They stayed up that first night talking, shutting down a less stuffy coffee house and then migrating to the living room of her apartment. She told him about college, her favorite classes, her struggle to register during the first year, dorm life, and the astronomical cost of a liberal arts education. He talked about run down theaters, open mike nights, coffee houses, house parties, using a fake ID to sneak into bars to play shows rather than drink, and overly anxious caffeine addicts. Different people they'd met along the way were described; somehow, Terry wasn't part of the conversation.

At two that morning, the old friends found themselves sitting on the floor, sharing a blanket. Their eyes met, they held hands beneath the blanket, and they kissed. The embrace seemed natural, without the awkward quality of most first kisses.

As the passion of their embrace picked up steam, Linea abruptly broke away. She excused herself, saying she worked in the morning but he was welcome to sleep there and stay until bus service resumed. Then Linea disappeared into her bedroom, closing the door behind her. Left alone to wonder what'd happened, Morgan slept in the bathtub and slunk off in the morning, without saying goodbye. As an afterthought, he left a note with his number and the time and location of his next gig.

Morgan didn't know what to expect after his initial encounter with Linea. He wished he could call her, maybe apologize for the kiss. But did he really have anything to apologize for? He was fairly certain that the kiss was mutual. Regardless, he didn't have her number. The only way he could be sure to see her again would be to drop by her apartment. Not knowing where he stood, Morgan decided against an unexpected visit.

He uneasily awaited his upcoming gig, wondering if she'd be in the audience. Janet Reno and the Somethings were playing at a lounge near the University of Washington. It was a pretty typical booking; one of six bands allotted thirty minutes to wow drunken college students. A good response would open the door to regular bookings in bars, lounges, and theaters around the University District. Success would also mean saying good-bye to the claustrophobic coffee house scene. Despite the implications of the show, Morgan remained preoccupied with Linea.

Janet Reno and the Somethings took the stage third, middle of the pack, a respectable placement for a relatively new group. Morgan was clicking on all cylinders that night, the performance a welcome distraction from his rattled nerves. His fat-body strat seemed like an extension of his body, as he effortlessly shredded his way through the set list. The entire band swaggered about the stage, following

Morgan's lead as he belted each song into the microphone with a cocked head and rhythmic flips of his blonde locks.

Halfway into their set, Morgan noticed someone pushing to the front of the crowd. Linea stood to the right of center stage. The group mellowed for the next song, one Morgan had written that week. A simple song about the work that goes into building and maintaining a relationship. About a man struggling to write a song that accurately reflected his feelings. A man that couldn't find the words to say he loved her. For this number alone, Morgan stopped his head bobs and hair flips. Instead, he performed only for Linea, not taking his eyes off her as he sang.

Back stage after the set, the band teemed with excitement over their performance. Morgan completely forgot about his inner turmoil over Linea. The stage manager came over, said there was someone who wanted to talk to him, as he continued to relish the roar of the crowd. The band stood dumbstruck, hoping to be greeted by a club owner or record producer. Instead, Morgan found himself congratulated by Linea. She was as ecstatic about the band's performance as they were and offered to take him out to celebrate.

"Not cool, dude," the rest of the band shouted after them.

They hadn't spoken in over a week. As the pair shared a meal at Cedars, their conversation was forced; neither wanted to address the awkward tension between them. At the end of the night, she gave him her number; they hugged, and sheepishly kissed each other on the cheek at a bus stop, ready to head in opposite directions. Morgan feared that he might not see her again.

At the last minute, Linea grabbed Morgan's hand, to prevent him from getting on the bus. She pulled him back.

"Did you write that song for me?"

Morgan nodded.

"I don't want you to go. I want you to come back with me," she said.

Morgan reached out, gently caressing Linea's chin. They kissed again and this time when they broke their embrace there were no abrupt goodnights.

She led him by the hand, onto her bus, and up to her place.

Gradually their relationship unfurled, as they rediscovered one another. A month into their blissful tryst, Morgan finally learned his true position in her life. He knew that the signs had been all around him. The picture of Linea embracing a guy who was not her brother on her mantel. Her reluctance to meet him anywhere in the University District. The random male socks in the laundry, when he wasn't allowed to leave anything behind. But he was too blindsided by love, too wrapped up in the fulfillment of his adolescent fantasies. So he pushed forward, following her siren song, a voluntary participant in their shared charade.

###

A block from his apartment, Morgan sat on the stoop of a closed law office. The street was quiet, with only an occasional drunkard passing by on his way to another bar. Sitting on the steps, Morgan looked up to the night sky. He hoped to see some stars, but knew that was impossible through the city's light pollution. Above him the overcast sky reflected the urban lights, lights that represented thousands of people, crammed into high-rise buildings, sprawled across suburban neighborhoods. Surrounded by people, Morgan felt alone.

He knew that he loved Linea. Shouldn't that be the only thing that mattered? She was compassionate, smart and beautiful. Morgan couldn't wait to see what she did with her life and wanted to be a part of it. He'd miss her nagging him about homeopathic medicine, her attempts to slip him Echinacea or fish oil tablets. The way she cheated at pool, leaning over the table in a low cut shirt. The watercolors and pastels she kept tucked in his closet. The way she insisted he take it slow during sex, no matter the time restraints.

But he also knew that he idealized her. Their relationship was built on deception and stolen time. Despite his resentment toward Terry, Morgan couldn't forget that he himself was the other man. He could never decide which was worse, to be the cheater and know about the other person, or to be the fool, lied to and believing everything was all right.

Linea was sure that Terry had no suspicions about Morgan, and she worked hard to keep it that way. When they met at parties, she would keep clear of Morgan, or treat him with the aloofness of an acquaintance. Morgan wondered if Terry was the only one being deceived.

This wasn't the first time he'd tried to break it off. And every time it was the same old story, tears, promises, declarations of love, and occasionally even resolutions that she'd leave Terry, when the time was right. The time was never right and the situation never changed. But still he believed her.

Morgan rose from the stoop and began walking back toward his apartment complex. Images stirred and mingled in his mind. Linea's swinging shoulder as she turned her back on him in the presence of her college friends. Linea lip-syncing in front of the stage at a show. Linea and Terry with their arms linked. Linea puttering about his apartment, trying in vain to create some order in the chaotic clutter. Was he in love with her? Or the idea of her?

At his door for the second time that night, Morgan hesitated. He knew that someday he'd have to fight for Linea, if he wanted to keep her in his life. Perhaps even force her hand. But not now. "I'll stay until she goes," he said to himself, as he turned the knob and entered the apartment.

Redd

The life cycle of the salmon is a common topic in schools around Washington state. Karen learned about their fatal migration growing up in the Skagit Valley, around the same time her husband Jake studied their Columbia River struggles in Vancouver. Karen remembered painting the salmon species of her choice in fourth grade. She'd painted a sockeye, with its distinctive humped back, garish red sides and hooked jaw. The final product resembled an exaggerated caricature more than the actual creature. Her mother had hung it on the refrigerator for a season before relegating it to a box in the attic with other touchstone school projects, essays, awards and other art projects. Karen wondered if her sockeye was still there.

For Jake, these annual studies of the salmon included multiple field trips to the Bonneville Dam fish ladder and the hatcheries along the Columbia's tributaries. He'd told Karen that the fish ladder could be viewed both from above, through cascades of water rapidly descending deep steps to simulate waterfalls, or through submerged windows below the churning surface. From the outside, eager visitors watch the water for the fish to jump as they ascend their aquatic switchbacks. From the inside, they press against the glass for a more consistent view of the fish. A pale, green-blue light filters through the windows as the fish swim by. "Though we seldom saw anything other than creepy, window-sucking lamprey," Jake recalled.

Karen mused on these descriptions while finishing her pregnancy during Vancouver's unprecedented heatwave. The metro area experienced three consecutive triple digit days for the first time in its recorded history, shattering the area's previous record high set in 1952. Her co-workers at OHSU constantly grumbled about the weather. Grace was the most consistent complainer. "I left Texas because of the heat," she'd moan to anyone who walked by, fanning herself in the records room.

Karen had never minded the rare summer heat. In fact, after a December family vacation to Orlando in her youth, she coveted warm weather. Convinced that such climates were foundations for happiness, she dreamed of escaping to sunny Florida to work as a marine biologist. Between SeaWorld and *Free Willy,* she'd fallen in love with orcas, even still had the Haida whale promotional necklace from the VHS at the bottom of her jewelry box. There in the opposite corner of the country, she would mow her lawn in a bikini top, shorts and sneakers, a fine layer of humid moisture glistening on her skin, just a normal part of daily life.

But that was before she met and married Jake, when they both moved to Seattle for college. Before they'd moved back to Jake's hometown, before the recession and student loans made it impossible for them to remain in Seattle. Before she waddled into her last trimester during the hottest summer in Vancouver's recorded meteorological history. Still, even before all those simple twists of fate, Karen recognized that mowing her lawn in a bikini top, shorts and sneakers would get her labeled "high maintenance" in the Pacific Northwest.

Their new house, like most in the region, lacked air conditioning. A luxury deemed unnecessary and too expensive in their typically temperate climate. With both of them working again, the best Karen and Jake could do was close off the house and hope the temperature didn't rise too much while they were out. Unfortunately, their home did an amazing impersonation of an oven and proved prone to retaining heat. A formidable prospect when leaving their air-conditioned workplaces. And so, on the hottest day, Karen opted not to go straight home after work. With their first child's impending birth, she'd made a habit of working as many hours as she could, to help them survive the lean finances during maternity leave. For this reason, Jake didn't question when Karen called to let him know she'd be late and not to wait to eat with her. He was freelancing at nights anyway and was easily distracted and often preoccupied. *Leave him to his sorting and unpacking,* she thought as her car cut through the sweltering heat up the gorge toward the fish ladder.

Karen wasn't sure why she'd lied to Jake about what she was doing that evening. Nor was she certain she'd set out to deceive him when she called. Lie was too strong a word. She'd never claimed she was working late. Karen simply hadn't corrected Jake's incorrect assumption. Still, she wasn't just not working an extra shift, she left early that afternoon. But what difference did it make? Who did it hurt? No one, as far as Karen could tell. And if this was the extent of her subterfuge in her marriage, she told herself that Jake should feel grateful.

Karen bypassed the orientation desk at the visitor complex and took the elevator directly to the fish viewing room. She felt the temperature drop as the doors opened to the cavernous concrete room and breathed a deep sigh. A row of windows with wide wooden lips, worn from the elbows, hands, feet and seats of previous visitors, lined the wall and peered into the water below the surface. Faux white shutters were mounted directly into the concrete walls. She couldn't decide if these accoutrements served some functional purpose or, as she suspected, were purely ornamental. The muted green light filtered in through the water, just as Jake had described. Speckled silver steelhead languidly swam upstream while a few stubby shad frantically fought the current generated by the concrete labyrinth of the ladder. At times, the stouter fish looked dazed and disoriented to Karen. Slender lamprey slithered and suckered their way along the bottoms of the windows. Occasionally a summer sockeye passed, but they were few and far between.

The walls of the viewing room were painted with murals of salmon on their intrepid journey upstream. Interpretive panels recounted the indigenous belief that the salmon returned and died in order to sustain the people. Karen wondered if preservation was all there was to reproduction. The floor was covered with thick, plushy carpet in large segments of rich pink, maroon, and two shades of blue. She wanted to say the carpet's alternating colors were intentional, perhaps representing currents. But she couldn't shake the feeling that the floor had simply been constructed from remnants or patched with strategic partial replacements.

Karen practically had the dam to herself. Few others had thought to utilize the fish viewing room as a refuge from the heat, instead hunkering down in the woods (tinder dry and ready to burst at the slightest spark), or their homes, or taking to the water themselves. She skirted the edge of the other visitors, eager to prevent anyone from infringing on this small, strange indulgence. As the pregnancy had progressed, Karen discovered that strangers couldn't resist touching her belly. They either asked but didn't wait for a response, which certainly would have been no, or simply didn't ask and helped themselves to her swelling midsection. Like an obviously adopted child or a person with a facial scar, pregnancy she discovered was an intimate detail about her she had no choice but to disclose to anyone that looked at her. The condition could be observed without any specific context. Forcing a blurring of the line between her private and public life in a way Jake only minimally shared when they were seen together. It had never occurred to her that this invasion of her personal space and private life would be an issue. She'd never experienced anything like it, outside of a handsy, loquacious date.

She found a section with no fish gawkers and gingerly sat on the wooden ledge with her back against the window's concrete jamb. On the other side of the glass, a few fish swam past her head, while lamprey futilely attempted to cling to her stomach with their sucker mouths. The low light and temperature washed over Karen. She took pleasure in the goosebumps induced by the cool glass and her own sweat after so many sweltering days. She removed her shoes and allowed her feet to dangle just above the floor.

She'd left her phone behind in the car, which meant she was cut off from her life. Jake couldn't reach her behind the concrete confines of the fish ladder. Leave him to his sorting and unpacking, she thought. Let him figure out what to eat on his own. With a slight smile, Karen placed her hands on either side of her stomach, closed her eyes, and focused on her breathing.

She honestly didn't expect Jake to try to check up on her. As far as he was concerned, she was safe at the office and would come home whenever she was ready. He'd be more concerned with putting his home office together than her whereabouts or well-being. It was no secret Jake wasn't happy about the pregnancy. He'd been withdrawn since learning that he would be a father. A sour aura seemed to permeate their life together, as though he blamed her for the return to his hometown, for the need to purchase the house. At best, it felt to Karen as though they were going through the motions with one another. She wondered if marriage was supposed to be this hard. She hoped an evening apart would do them both good.

Karen wasn't thrilled with the situation either. While her connections and the promise of a job at OHSU had facilitated the move, they could have found a way to stay in Seattle. The move took her farther from her own familial support system in the Skagit Valley.

She realized how bad the timing was, even though kids were part of their plan. Initially she hadn't even told Jake about the pregnancy. She recognized how disruptive it would be and considered terminating it without telling him. She'd gone so far as to find a clinic that would handle things discreetly. After all it was her body, her choice, right? And what Jake didn't know wouldn't hurt him. They could continue to finally get their life back on track. Things weren't perfect, but it felt like they were making progress together again. The pregnancy was the latest in a series of unexpected complications that had plagued them since entering the adult world.

In the end, in the lonely waiting room of the clinic, Karen had thought better of it. It was his child too, and she wasn't sure inconvenience was a good enough reason when they did eventually want kids. However irrational it may have been, she feared she might never be able to get pregnant again. Once she'd told him and their families, there was no going back. The choice was made and the pregnancy would naturally run its course. Jake did put in some effort, attending birthing classes, driving her to doctor's appointments, and reading parenting books with her. The exaggerated effort he put into ensuring the most convenient bathroom remained available to her always made her smile. But all of these tasks were performed with a sense of duty and obligation, not loving enthusiasm. Jake also did more than his fair share of sulking, as though he'd been trapped by some biological trick, while she bore the physical, social and financial burdens.

Their parents were ecstatic which added the strain of putting on a happy and brave face to Karen. The pressure increasingly left her exhausted. Despite the general excitement around the announcement and her own resignation to move forward, Karen still wasn't sure at times that she'd made the right decision.

She felt the gentle pressure of an extra set of digits on the center of her stomach. When Karen opened her eyes, she was face to face with a park ranger. Her long, silver hair was braided and tucked beneath her flat hat. The other visitors were gone. The ranger perched next to her on the landing, and for a moment it felt like they were a pair of thirteen-year-olds sitting side-by-side on the floor by a bed just trying to figure everything out. Karen shifted awkwardly and prepared for the typical onslaught of questions---when she was due, is this your first baby. Instead, the ranger smiled and told her she was carrying a healthy, baby girl. When Karen asked how the ranger knew, she said "instinct." And with that, the ranger let her know the visitor center would be closing in twenty-minutes, and left Karen to enjoy her temperate refuge.

She wasn't sure if she could or wanted to believe the ranger. Until that moment, Karen hadn't put a lot of thought into the gender of the child. In many ways the baby felt like an extension of herself. Even Jake viewed the baby as part of her. The ranger's prognostication added weight to the situation. A child, kids, had remained an abstract concept. Something reserved for the mythic someday. Karen had never considered a preference toward a son or daughter. Why did it matter? What could she do with one but not the other? Although plenty of people, including her own mother, advised her to hope for a boy. They claimed boys were "easier" to raise, whatever that meant. Karen just wanted the child to be healthy and happy. She had no grand plans for her offspring other than to raise her to be a decent human being. Karen didn't want her daughter to live as an ornament or means for her to vicariously recapture her youth. Such intentions felt like narcissism that could only lead to impossible expectations and strained relationships. For the first time, however, she wondered if Jake had any preferences. They hadn't had a chance to discuss the practical elements of raising a child. Would he be disappointed in his daughter?

Karen crammed her swollen feet back into her shoes and turned to consider the fish one last time. Despite everything people knew about them, salmon were still mysterious. No one knew how salmon find their way back to their home redds, to the streams of their birth. Instinct? Scent? Magnets? Some combination? The salmon were drawn on despite the obstacles, by the need to reproduce, to pass on their genes, guarantee the survival of their species. And then die.

She knew not all of them would make it. Some would fail to find the safe way past the dam. Others would get picked off by the opportunistic sea lions and birds that waited for them to bottleneck at the ladder's entrance. There were many tributaries upriver that hadn't seen a single salmon in decades. Karen pressed her back against the cool glass one last time, her hands lightly resting on her stomach. She felt for the little tremors that represented the life within, as a rare run of summer sockeye with bright red sides swam against the current behind her.

And she wondered how much longer their lives would be if they chose to keep living in the ocean and never have sex.

Goodnight, Irene

Irene's first call on the landline came three months into Karen's pregnancy. We had just moved into the house in Hazel Dell. The cordless phone stood erect, a black monolith suddenly alive on the filing cabinet. The artificial tones and blue light intruded on my tiny home office. Surprised out of checking soccer scores at my desk, I backhanded the receiver from its stand.

It was our first white pages listing together, a milestone that didn't excite Karen. She questioned why I wanted the landline. We both had cell phones, just like everyone else we knew. The best justification I could come up with was feigned paranoia: "When the government hits us with the electromagnetic pulse, I don't want to be cut off."

She laughed. "But Jake, we'll still be cut off, with the only landline in existence by then." We were both working again and the monthly charge wasn't exactly a budget buster, especially with the cable company pushing their tv-internet bundle, so she ultimately let the subject drop.

The truth was I had a certain amount of nostalgia for phones grounded in a place. When I was a teenager, my parents had installed a second line in the house for me and my older brother. The folks eventually dedicated the number to their dial up Internet. But the summer I let Irene dye my hair blue, that phone was ours, the best way to reach us.

That second line filled us with a sense of independence and maturity, like swearing in middle school. We bought our own unique receiver, a scale model of a VW Beetle convertible. The headlights lit up when it rang, a high-pitched sound more like an air compressor than a bell. Late at night, I would turn off the ringer and watch for the lights. On the other end, Irene would speak in hushed tones, tucked away in a closet with her cordless.

We bought our own answering machine and recorded funny messages with fake beeps and popular song parodies. Things we never could've done on the family answering machine. Our most popular message was set to the tune of Green Day's "Good Riddance." I picked away on the guitar while my brother nasally sang: *Another person calls while I'm away from home. So leave your name, number, and a message after the tone. Let's make the most of this answering machine of mine; I'll call you back when I have the time.* Girls who wouldn't talk to me at school would call just to hear that one. Irene was disappointed when we finally replaced it with the Joey Scarbury's "Believe It or Not."

The first call came around 11:00 on a Friday night. I was holed up in the office, while Karen continued her campaign to put our house in order. I was listening to the type of music she didn't really enjoy, like The Vandals and Pennywise, when the phone started ringing.

Although I had adjusted the volume during installation, I hadn't heard the phone ring since. The electronic sound was startling and harsh, not like the techno-beats, guitar riffs, or song clips available on a cell phone. I turned down my music, retrieved the receiver from the floor, and prepared myself for a telemarketer in India confused about time zones.

Her initial response to my answering was delayed, as if she was expecting a funny machine message. I could hear her breathing over muffled voices as though she was on the edge of a crowded room. I could barely make out a song in the background, "She Smiles Sweetly," by the Rolling Stones. She didn't say anything when I asked if anyone was there. I was about to hang up.

"Jake Wallace?" Her voice was scratchy and low, like it was outside the Crystal Ballroom, after we shouted and sang along with Reel Big Fish for two hours.

"Irene?" I said. "How the fuck are you? How was Sara Lawrence?"

"Turns out I wasn't as progressive as I thought," she said. "I moved back after the first semester."

"Why didn't I know that?"

"You kind of disappeared after graduation."

I told her I was just up in Seattle; she should've looked me up. It wasn't like I'd moved across the country and failed to tell anyone I'd returned. She got quiet after that, so I probably laid on the fake guilt trip too heavy. Irene wasn't catching my dry, sarcastic sense of humor like she did in the past, or maybe she'd just outgrown it. After another minute of breathing and background noise, I asked where she was.

"I'm at the Showboat Tavern. You should come out. We could have a private reunion."

Karen walked past the office, dragging a chair with a box on the seat toward the living room. She paused in the doorway, pointed at me and then the chair, before picking up the box and continuing on her way. "Ah, not tonight," I said. "It was good to hear from you but I've got to go. Goodnight, Irene."

When I emerged from the office, Karen was waiting in the living room. "Somebody actually call you on that dinosaur?" She eyed the arrangement of furniture with the balance of photos on the walls.

I started to tell her about Irene but found myself suddenly self-conscious. Nothing happened. Sure, Irene and I used to date but that was years ago. But why didn't she tell me when she came back? Why contact me now after all these years? I decided it was all probably nothing and so not worth getting into a lengthy explanation with Karen over. "Wrong number," I said. "What needs to be moved?"

Karen and I had moved back to Vancouver, Washington after I lost my job in Seattle. She found work at OHSU in transcription, while I scrounged around for opportunities at local advertising firms. Ironically, my next job appeared when I filed my unemployment claim at the Vancouver WorkSource office. A week later, I was working for the re-employment section of the Department of Employment Security. I taught classes on writing and formatting resumes, and counseled others on professional interview techniques. Who better to help those looking for work to market their skills than an ex-advertising agent?

Before I got laid off, Karen had been talking about having kids, even seen a few doctors. We started tracking ovulation cycles, researching school districts and looking at houses in Ballard. But I begged her to go back on her pills once my job disappeared. She was hurt, but I promised we'd try again once things settled down. When she actually got pregnant while I was still in my probationary period with the state, things didn't get any more relaxed.

A month went by before the phone rang again. I had forgotten the whole awkward incident with Irene. It wasn't late, but Karen and I were already in bed. Jarred from sleep by the shrill sound, I blinked in the darkness until my mind recalibrated. Karen rolled and placed her hand lightly on my chest. "What is that?" she mumbled, still half asleep.

"The phone. Go back to sleep." I gently kissed her on the forehead, rolled her back over, and got up, closing the door behind me. In the office I sat at my desk and waited another couple rings, thinking whoever it was would hang up. But no luck, the phone kept insisting I answer. Finally, I grabbed the receiver and clicked it on.

"Happy Hump Day." Her voice brought the previous call back to me. The second call lacked the background noise of the first. She was obviously somewhere more private, probably home. It was hard to say.

"Do you know what time it is?" I asked.

"Of course, I've got a watch," she said. "Do you know what I'm wearing?"

"What? No."

"You used to be so good at guessing what panties a girl was wearing. That skill must not improve with age."

"Guess not." I rubbed my eye with the palm of my hand.

"Silk stockings, with garters---"

"What?"

"What I'm wearing. I remember stockings used to get you hard in a hurry. And no guy in school could unhook a bra faster than you."

"Yeah, and you always did have demanding boobs, starved for attention." What was I saying? I was beginning to enjoy the exchange. And Irene didn't miss a beat.

"They could use some attention now."

"I'm married."

"I don't mind."

"Goodnight, Irene."

I hung up the phone and remained at my desk for a moment. Was this the sort of thing you told your wife about? Or was it better left unsaid? Nothing had happened, at least not on my part. I had nothing to hide, right? Either way I could see where it might cause a fight. I slunk back to the bedroom, unsure what to say if questioned. Fortunately, Karen wasn't awake when I got back in bed.

The next day after work, while Karen was at the store, I pulled out my old high school yearbooks from a box in the closet. Laid them out across the desk, all opened to Irene's picture. In each she had the same half smile and intense stare. Only her clothes, hair length and color, and amount of eye makeup varied. I remembered how in sophomore biology she'd sit across from me and give me the same half smile before slipping her foot out of her shoe, sliding it between my legs to massage my junk with her toes. We formed a band together that same year. She always gyrated through practice with her guitar firmly pressed against her hip. She'd toss her hair and sway to the rhythm in a plaid miniskirt and an Everclear t-shirt. She'd even arranged our biggest gig, one night only opening for Animatronic Cowboy at the Aladdin Theater, the single high point of our music "career." In those days anything felt possible with Irene.

I got online and searched her name. But the results weren't promising. Public records stuff. And a link to an old *Columbian* article about her acceptance to Sara Lawrence. No social or professional networking profiles. No videos or pictures. Irene's virtual presence was almost suspiciously absent. I wondered what she knew about me, who did she think I was?

I began to feel like there were too many Jakes. There was Karen's Jake, dependable, affectionate, spending his weekends doing yard work, baby proofing the house and watching soccer. Office Jake, professional, a friendly coworker, but reserved about his home life.

But Irene was calling Teenage Jake, in a punk band with velvet blue hair and an offbeat sense of humor. She wanted him to sneak out with his friends, to view the hanging tree at midnight. To float the Washougal River on a summer day, Irene in a red bikini with matching lipstick. To drive over to Portland for a concert and donuts. My brother jabbed the pretzel cross into Donut Woman, as red jelly oozed from her belly. He asked Irene if she knew you could get married in the shop. She bit her lip and diverted her gaze to the Memphis Mafia we were sharing, before she slugged me in the arm and told him she did.

Was Teenage Jake even still around? Did everyone live such fractured lives? It seemed overly complicated and fragile. Like these various compartmentalized aspects of my life had to remain separate, that if they were to overlap at all, they would collapse in on themselves. Exposing what, I wasn't sure.

The next day at work, I decided to see how others would react to Irene's Jake. My manager called me into her cube to discuss the proper protocols for handling a disgruntled client. Specifically, the question was what to do if someone approached you with a gun at the front desk. The week had been filled with threatening phone calls.

I sat across from her in her pantsuit. I was dressed slightly more casually than normal, with my hair gelled into a sort of faux hawk. Karen had teased me on my way out that morning, wanted to know where I was meeting Sid Vicious for lunch.

My supervisor tapped her pencil and waited for my answer. "Ask the client to step outside and to please read the sign at the front door," I said. "It clearly states no food, drinks, or weapons." She failed to see the humor in my response, since the correct answer was to sit still and wait for security. Try not to provoke them.

She was even less impressed with my suggestion that we hang a large banner declaring *We Don't Have Any Money,* to deter robbers. She shook her head and told me she hoped I took my classes more seriously than I did security, and dismissed Teenage Jake.

A week later, Irene called again. Karen was at the Y taking a water aerobics class for pregnant women. She wanted to get back in shape quickly after giving birth. I was on edge, like something was pricking me. If Karen noticed she didn't acknowledge it. We got along fine and continued to settle into our new home and prepare for the baby.

A little less restrained, I decided to let Irene talk. Figured I would let her get whatever this was out of her system and that would be the end of the whole affair. She'd just gotten out of the shower. The evening was warm, but the spring breezes felt good on her still damp skin and gave her goosebumps.

"Close your eyes," she said. "Are they closed?"

"Mhmmm."

"What do you think my bush is like?"

I tried to picture Irene. She sat on the edge of a bed, a towel wrapped loosely around her. Goosebumps dotted the pale skin of her arms and legs like Braille. "Shaved," I said. "Am I right?"

"Come see for yourself. I'll meet you at Showboat."

I opened my eyes and saw the picture of Karen on my desk. The excitement I felt sank to the pit of my stomach and turned to sour guilt. I hung up the phone.

I sat there a minute, staring at the ceiling. And then I was putting on my shoes, grabbing my keys and driving out to the bar. I didn't go in, just sat in the parking lot and watched the entrance. If she showed up, I didn't recognize her.

After a half hour, I drove home, stopping at the store to grab some odds and ends to justify my absence to Karen. I felt more shaken this time. I'd definitely participated in Irene's games. I knew that I hadn't cheated on my wife, and was fairly certain I had no plans to. I told myself it was no different than checking a woman out at the store, harmless. Even going to the bar, I didn't really want to meet Irene. I just wanted to see her, was curious about a woman from my past. Still, I couldn't deny that I'd crossed a line.

The calls kept coming, every week or so. Karen grew suspicious when she noticed the timing of the calls. The best I could do was say it was an old friend, which wasn't a total lie. We'd been in a band together and dated in high school. Both broke up when college took us in different directions. I moved to Seattle and met Karen. And Irene was supposed to go off to New York and never come back, not call and invite me for drinks.

What else could I tell her? I knew I wouldn't be thrilled to learn that Karen had been having late night chats that bordered on phone sex with one of her ex-boyfriends. Karen seemed to accept my excuses, but only asked if my friend could at least call at a more reasonable hour.

I started seeing Irene everywhere. Bagging my groceries. Waiting in the Work First line at the office. Jogging through our neighborhood when I went to check the mail. Not really, but I feared running into her. The last time I'd actually seen her, she was 17. My underage mental image of her made my part in our encounters feel even dirtier.

The only justification I gave myself for my poor behavior was that nothing had physically taken place. I'd never cheated on anyone and didn't intend to start with my wife. Still, I worried that the only thing between infidelity and me was distance.

And Irene was relentless, even trying to convince me one night that I was the only one who could give her a ride home from the bar. She told me it would be worth my while and that if I didn't some other guy would probably try to play grab ass with her in his truck. And I wouldn't like that, would I? And the truth was I wouldn't. As she talked my jaw clenched tighter with each word, before she finally hung up on me. I put on my shoes and stared at the phone, ready to tell her I was on my way, if she would just call back. But the phone remained silent.

During the last few weeks of her pregnancy, Karen worked late, tying up loose ends before her leave and increasing our savings. There was no overtime at my office, so I was freelancing from home in the evenings for advertising agencies in Portland.

After Irene hung up on me, I decided to follow the state's policy of security through inaction. I resolved not to answer the phone after 8:00 p.m. I was on my computer, attempting to increase the online presence of a local bakery, when the phone rang. I checked the clock, it was 6:30 p.m. I told myself maybe Karen was calling from the hospital to give me an update on when she would be back, and to rib me about still holding onto this line. I should've known better, but I felt compelled to answer.

"You're getting pretty hard to get ahold of."

"Been busy. In fact, I'm in the middle of something right now."

"Can't it wait?"

I hesitated. "What do you want?"

"You know what I want."

I saved my work and shifted my chair toward the window. Reminded Irene that I was married. And she reminded me that she didn't care. "I'll put on the fishnets and a plaid skirt for old time's sake. Please, Jake." She placed a hollow, breathy emphasis on the please. But still, I refused to see her and asked her to stop calling.

"You can't tell me you haven't enjoyed our conversations," she said.

I felt my cheeks flush and was glad Irene couldn't see me. She wasn't wrong. There was a certain thrill I felt from our lewd phone calls. I hadn't always felt that rush with Karen since we started trying to have kids. I still loved Karen but our sex life had become stagnant and transactional. I looked at the picture of Karen on my desk and told myself all of that was just nerves. I wasn't going to be one of those men that used pregnancy as an excuse to cheat. "I can't do this anymore."

Irene got pretty upset after that. She begged me to stay on the phone. Said we could do everything I wanted, if I just came to see her. When I still wouldn't take the bait, she questioned my sexuality, even unloaded a string of homophobic slurs. Called my wife a controlling cunt, then threatened to kill herself if I hung up.

"I'm not fucking around," she said. "If you hang up, I'll drive down to the river. Throw myself in and drown."

I didn't know what else to do or say. "I'm sorry. Take care, Irene."

That was the last time I heard from her. The phone went silent. I'd be lying if I said I didn't miss the calls. Our relaxed sexual talk. The thrill of concealment. I can't deny I felt guilty. A couple nights after work I even drove out to Showboat, sat in the back and kept an eye out for Irene. I still didn't want to meet her, just wanted to see that she was all right. Plenty of women came to the tavern, a few even approached me in my dark booth. But none of them were Irene.

I searched the newspapers, but there were no reports of a woman being pulled out of any local rivers, no mention of her name, and no obituary. I tried to inquire about her with old friends. But no one had kept in touch with Irene, or seen her since high school. The most I got was that our old bass player's cousin had taken a history class with Irene at Lewis and Clark. He didn't know if she'd graduated or not. Despite our conversations, I'd never learned anything about her present life. Irene vanished, as if she'd never existed, just a phantom of my own guilt. But as the months passed, other things crowded her out of my mind.

Karen had our little girl, Lena. When she was three months old, Lena developed a nasty cold. I spent all night walking her around the living room. She'd only sleep while tilted in someone's arms and on the move. Exhausted from walking her all day, Karen was asleep in the bedroom. So, I bounced her, and spoke to her softly. What else could I do?

Each time I passed the office, the silent phone caught my eye. Was that seventeen-year-old in fishnets still alive? I longed for the phone to ring, as much as I longed for Lena's fever to break. I wondered what Irene was doing. What was she wearing? Had she disappeared from our time after I hung up that phone? Was I responsible? She would never be able to imagine what I was doing. I smiled and brushed Lena's hair with my hand and kissed her burning forehead. I stood next to the window. Outside the moon was full, but tomorrow it would start waning. "Goodnight, Irene. I'll see you in my dreams," I whispered as I unplugged the phone.

The Dispatched

By midday, Caleb had no idea where his crew was, but he knew they weren't in Ottie's watermelon patch. The low vines that crept along the soil in search of water offered no relief from the sun. A man who tried to lie beneath that leathery ground cover would find nothing but sunburn. Caleb didn't have to check to know that the broad leaves concealed only melons and panting rabbits.

He knelt for a moment by the edge of the plants and felt the coarse under fur of the leaves between his fingers, prickly and soft at the same time. Above him loomed a series of sprinklers mounted on posts. The patch was kept lush through generous irrigation. Left to the heat of July the vines would vanish, just like his crew, beneath the relentless sun.

His first summer in Hermiston, a drought had devastated the small garden his mother planted behind their trailer. The county didn't allow watering in their area. Still, she made him kneel on the hard soil with her each morning while she tried to salvage the remains. They vainly tended the shriveled plants, unwilling to give up on the promise of the fresh tomatoes, green beans and corn that surrounded them, and that they could not afford to buy. But without water, the effort was useless.

The early afternoon heat scorched the earth around his feet as Caleb surveyed Ottie's patch. He wiped his brow with a handkerchief from his pocket and absently scanned the horizon for his missing crew. The ground south of the field, blemished with the stubs of last year's vines, looked barren and dead. Clouds of dust wafted up from the land with even the slightest of summer breezes. Nothing else stirred out there in the rippling air.

Caleb had been promoted to foreman three seasons ago, when Ottie discovered his two years of high school Spanish. In theory, he could communicate all of the old man's wishes and jokes to the field hands. His work around the farm was now less strenuous, but Caleb found the managerial position exhausting. He should have asked to drive the delivery truck to Portland instead. Leave early every morning, with Woody Guthrie crackling through the speakers. Watch the sunrise illuminating the city's skyline. Chat up the suppliers and enjoy the streets teeming with life, not dust. Alone in the cab for hours, he would be responsible only for himself, not worrying about the labor of other men, or the productivity of someone else's land.

The farm's stand stood in the distance, a faded pole building stained by the red dust blown against it, situated just off the gravel service road. There were no windows, just screened openings covered by shutters when the wind kicked up in the afternoon. As trucks passed the junction of I-84 and I-82, they rattled the stand so violently you'd swear they were coming through the back at any moment.

Cars of families stopped, enticed by Ottie's big wooden sign shaped like a large watermelon slice. Season after season, Caleb watched as husbands and wives argued in hushed tones, carrying on disagreements that had started miles away. Women eyed the Honey Buckets and tried to decide if they could hold out for the next stop. Their children ran about the stand, kicking rocks and tracking grasshoppers.

Ottie's daughter Lauren would be in the stand now, sitting on a cooler and fanning herself. He pictured her strawberry blonde hair pulled tightly in a braid, its tip resting at the nape of her neck. Her freckles had faded over the years, or she concealed them with makeup, he wasn't sure which. Caleb remembered when she was a shy 10-year-old in pigtails. He had been a gangly, 16-year-old kid when he started to work for Ottie. Back then, if she didn't have her nose stuck in a book, she was holding picnics with her stuffed animals on the dried lawn. She called him Beanpole, mimicking her father.

Periodically, Lauren would cut new, sweet triangles from a melon stashed in the cooler, and pile them on a tray near the register. She would talk with the customers and help them select a good melon, making a show of placing her ear on the variegated shell and knocking, before ringing up their purchases. For large stretches of the day her only duty was to sit and listen to the highway. Behind her, rows of melons picked fresh that morning stretched out on wooden tiers, as if the fruit were sitting in a grandstand watching her perform.

In the fall she would return to college in Eugene. Ottie boasted that his little girl was going to get a business degree, then come back and run the farm with him. But Ottie could have taught her everything she needed to know. Besides, Caleb doubted that Lauren had even a passing interest in presiding over the watermelon patch and roadside stand. He suspected she had more ambition than that.

Caleb remembered his own attempt to get out. He was on spring break from high school, and out to prove the guidance counselor wrong. *Join the army*, she advised Caleb, *or you'll never amount to anything more than a field hand. And you'll never leave Hermiston.*

Hitchhiking and hoofing, he made it as far west as Memaloose State Park the first night. Still early in the season, the place was deserted except for the ranger waiting to take campsite deposits. He leaned out the window of his booth, watching as Caleb walked around the outer rest stop. Nervous that the ranger might call a highway patrolman, Caleb decided not to linger near the road. Looking back on it now, he wondered why he thought the ranger would care. No one in Hermiston had even noticed he was gone.

Instead of staying in the park, he'd made his way to the railroad tracks that hugged the bank of the Columbia River. He stood near the water and marveled at Memaloose Island. It looked like a body lying on its side, legs bent at the knees. He'd learned in school that the island was an Indian burial site, and he wondered how many spirits were in the air, spirits of people who hadn't tied themselves to one place, who wandered the land freely as they followed each passing season, with no one telling them their limits. He had laughed. Even then, Caleb knew that was all movie Indian bullshit.

Freight trains came by his camp and he considered hopping one. But none ever passed slowly enough to allow him to overcome his fear and leap. They rumbled through without him on their way to Portland. Caleb sat in the brush and watched the flickering body of Memaloose through the gaps in the grain cars. The shadowy images of the river reminded him of those old grainy filmstrips he'd watched in school about the promise of hydroelectric power.

The next morning, cold and hungry, Caleb pennied the tracks as he had when he was six years old. Then he admitted defeat and returned to Hermiston. He didn't meet with the counselor again, but registered for classes that might help him go on to trade school. He took a part time job at Ottie's that summer. Then his mother got sick, probably from water contaminated by Hanford nuclear waste, or Umatilla mustard gas. Or the pesticides he worked around every day. Soon his meager savings and plans to escape dried up faster than their first garden.

Caleb walked through the vines toward the stand. He avoided disturbing the melons. Dust kicked up with each step. The crew would need to irrigate this afternoon, before the vines collapsed and the fruit spoiled. He knew that the men would gravitate toward shade. Despite her father's intolerance for laziness, Lauren wouldn't run the field hands out of the stand. Caleb figured she enjoyed the attention, and why not? It wasn't her job to keep them on task.

As Caleb trudged through the melon patch, a jackrabbit leapt from beneath a clump of broad leaves, where he'd probably been resting and munching on new growth all morning. The rabbit population had exploded the last few seasons. Ottie had been on Caleb to keep the pests under control since spring. But the traps couldn't keep up with their numbers, and the stand and parking lot were too close to the field to use the more practical option of a shotgun. The big jack bounded down the row and glared back at him, as if *he* were trespassing.

"I'll deal with you later," Caleb said without conviction, and continued to the melon stand.

Lauren sat just as Caleb had imagined, except she was munching an egg salad sandwich she washed down with a Coke. A grimy box fan whirred in the doorway, moving the air in the building without cooling it. She didn't acknowledge Caleb's approach. He hoped she hadn't seen him coming, that her lack of interest didn't reflect her attention to the customers.

"Many cars stop today?" He had to raise his voice to be heard over the hum of the fan and the noise from the nearby highway.

She looked at him with one raised eyebrow, and finished her sandwich before answering. "A few, mostly the ones without air conditioning."

The Coke can perspired in her hand. Caleb watched the beads of water slide down the sides, only to be blocked by her fingers. Her right hand, newly freed from clasping the sandwich, began to drum on a book near the register. Her nails were painted a pale pink.

He'd asked her out last Thursday, a couple weeks after she'd come home. He thought they could grab dinner at Hale's. Then take a six-pack out to Hat Rock or check out the Farm City Pro Rodeo. They'd hung out in the past, never planned events, just spur of the moment things when they ran into each other in town. She always seemed like she'd had a good time. Caleb didn't see any reason he shouldn't ask.

The last Friday before she left for college, she rode up to Kennewick with him on an errand. On the way back they drove through the Umatilla refuge, and she asked him to stop by the river, near the slough boat ramp. Once the truck stopped, she unbuckled both their seat belts and pulled him away from the wheel. She'd straddled him in the cab. They kissed, and her hands firmly gripped either side of his face. Then she slid off him, undid his jeans and reached down into his shorts. When she was finished, she wiped her hand on his handkerchief. Neither of them spoke. Caleb fastened his jeans, got back behind the wheel and headed for Hermiston.

But last Thursday she already had plans to spend the weekend in Portland with some school friends. Not a definite no, until he suggested they go out some other time.

"I don't want you to get the wrong idea," she said. "I mean you're great and all, but we're not really an option." He thought he'd accepted the news well enough, hid his surprise, and played off any indication that the invitation was anything but a friendly joke. Still, she'd been distant since then, avoiding him around the place and offering short replies when they did speak.

Caleb waved his hand over the sample tray to discourage the flies and yellow jackets from loitering on the sweet juicy flesh. "Have you seen the guys?"

"They said they were going to work on the tiller."

Caleb thanked her and took one last look at her fingers. Lean and delicate, pianist's fingers. Fingers that didn't know work beyond pushing the buttons on a cash register or a keyboard. He doubted those fingers had washed a single dish. Lauren's mother had been lost during childbirth, and Ottie had always doted on his only child.

Caleb remembered how soft the unspoiled skin of Lauren's palms felt as he made his way to the barn. He clenched his own hands and listened to the crack of his knuckles. Both fists were covered with dried, cracked skin, worn and callused. Caleb wondered what his hands were worth. Could they still pluck chords from the guitar he tried to take up when he was thirteen? Would any woman care for the stroke of his rough palm?

An old John Deere cultivator rusted outside the barn. His approach scattered a doe and four baby bunnies huddled near its large back wheels. Several voices overlapped in the barn. Words flowed from Spanish tongues, faster than he could possibly hope to comprehend. But the exchange was brought to an abrupt conclusion as he entered.

Sanchez, Ernesto, Carlos, and Javier lounged on some bales of alfalfa stacked against the far wall. Out of the sun, their broad brimmed hats rested on their knees. Gabriel sat on the axle of the working tractor, a cloth in one hand and the oil dipstick dangling from the other. Caleb could just hear Ottie if he walked in on this scene. *I'm not running a goddamn social club. How many men does it take to check the oil in one tractor, for Christ's sake?* Although he could understand Ottie's frustration, he also understood the reality of working watermelons in 100 degree heat. Ottie hadn't been out in the fields since he was a boy, helping his own father. The men on the alfalfa fidgeted, as if they could avoid his gaze by burrowing themselves into the bales.

"Señor Caleb!" Gabriel rose from the axle and replaced the dipstick. He turned to smile at the foreman. "We came in here to eat lunch and decided to check on the equipment." Gabriel transitioned between tongues with ease.

The rest of the crew, now partially concealed in the alfalfa, tried to read Caleb's expression. He attempted to show no signs of amusement or flashes of anger. Keep an even keel, Caleb told himself; they couldn't have been in here for more than an hour. "What time did you guys start lunch?"

"*Mediodia.*"

Caleb looked at his watch. 1:15. He lingered on the watch, let Gabriel and the rest of the crew squirm for a minute. Only seventeen, Gabriel had already worked these fields for three seasons. He stood still, smiling at the foreman, oily dirt on his pants, dust streaked through his hair. If he was squirming he was doing a hell of a job hiding it. The other men remained tense, chins pressed into their necks. Their dark eyes were focused, unblinking. Gabriel had been here longer than most of them; experienced men usually avoided the stooping and lifting of watermelon season.

"As much as Ottie appreciates well maintained equipment, I think he needs y'all in the fields more," Caleb said, looking Gabriel in the eye. "Say you guys wrap this up and get back out there in the next five minutes. Pick the melons in the northwest patch and check the rabbit traps before you turn on the sprinklers. *Por favor.*"

The crew turned from Caleb to Gabriel. Gabriel translated and the barn was soon filled with a chorus of *Si señor, gracias.*

Caleb nodded to the men and turned for the door. Gabriel caught his arm. "Can I speak with you?"

The two men walked ten yards toward the stand. Across the road, turkey vultures circled a vacant field rotated out of planting. Caleb wondered if they'd found a rabbit, injured by one of the traps. Gabriel looked anxious, his smile forced, his hands shoved into his pockets.

"What's up?"

"As you know, *señor*, most of my wages go back to my mother's family in Chiapas. But I want to go to school and become a lawyer. I enrolled at the community college. They're offering some help, but not enough. Do you think Mr. Ottie would assist me?"

He watched Gabriel kick at the dirt, showing more nerves than he had in the barn. "You mean like a loan?"

"I promise to pay him back. I'll work as many summers as I have to. I thought you could ask him for me."

Caleb ran his tongue along his teeth. He wasn't surprised by the request, the kid was bright enough, and since his return this season he'd seemed restless. Usually, he spent his breaks reading books, rather than bullshitting with the other hands. "Why not ask him yourself?"

Gabriel laughed. "*Señor* Ottie hardly knows who I am, and always speaks to me like I don't understand English."

"What makes you think I can convince him?" Caleb pointed back at the barn. "Why not ask Ernesto?"

"Because you've known him longer. He trusts you."

"Yeah, he trusts me enough not to give me a raise in nearly ten years."

"Please *señor*. I want to get out of the migrant labor camp."

Caleb thought of his own childhood as a migrant. His father had been a gyppo logger, and he spent his first six years in platform tents outside Klamath Falls. When the price of timber fell, they ate grouse or venison, sometimes fish with potatoes, and wild berries when they were in season. He could still taste the berries, small and tart, not like the bland ones shipped up from California in early spring. After a falling limb killed his father, his mother took a job as a short order cook in Hermiston. He'd been here ever since.

"I'll see what I can do." Caleb extended his hand to Gabriel.

"*Gracias señor.*" Gabriel looked surprised by the gesture, but he shook the hand with vigor.

"I'm not making any promises."

"*Si,* I understand sir."

"Once you get the guys picking again, what do you say you go relieve Lauren in the stand for the rest of the day?"

"*Gracias.*" A wide grin broke out on Gabriel's face as he trotted back into the barn to reorganize the crew.

Once the men resumed work, Gabriel cleaned up and settled in next to Lauren behind the counter in the stand. There was always a lull in traffic during the odd hours between lunch and the evening commute. A few customers trickled in, but Gabriel would see little business. Caleb checked on the men in the northwest patch, stooped over them and urged them in broken Spanish to be more careful with the melons. Satisfied that they knew he was keeping track of their work, he withdrew to the south patch.

Carefully, Caleb cleaned and baited the traps. The spring-loaded steel jaws were chained to the ground at intervals in the center and along the periphery of each field. The only sections not booby-trapped were the edges near the parking lot and stand. The traps were simple, and quickly fatal when a rabbit entered headfirst. The more unfortunate rabbits got snared by the haunches and died slowly, or waited for Caleb to deliver the final blow.

Ottie wanted the rabbits gone but was clear he didn't want their bodies left around. The odor of the carcasses might attract coyotes. Caleb didn't understand this objection; a small pack could've snuffed out the rabbit problem in no time. And once the rabbits were gone, the coyotes would move along.

But Ottie didn't see it that way, and he wasn't running a goddamn wildlife preserve. So the old man insisted that the dispatched be dealt with in two ways. Those caught alive or freshly killed by the traps were boiled for the hounds. Caleb hated smashing their skulls or slitting their throats. The ones caught in the perimeter snares, necks broken or feet caught, were usually too spoiled by the time they were discovered. Their bodies were locked away in a trashcan near the shed, where they festered until Caleb could burn them in the evening.

With the traps cleaned and reset, Caleb decided to check in with Ottie. In a gunnysack he carried three fresh carcasses that needed to be boiled. The old farmhouse sat back from the road, in the middle of the quarter section. Caleb walked up the gravel driveway; he had cleared it of snow, or sprayed it for weeds in summer, countless times over the years. Lauren's blue Beetle convertible was parked outside. The car was a high school graduation present. Ottie didn't want his little girl to have any excuse not to come home from Eugene. But Caleb figured the car made more trips to Portland than it ever did to Hermiston.

He'd been to Portland when he'd filled in for the truck driver. Gotten lunch from a food cart in the Pearl and seen the type of men Lauren spent her weekends with. Guys in pea coats, tight jeans and thick-rimmed glasses, their hair combed over one eye. Scrawny and pale, they'd sleep until noon and work part time in a café or bike shop.

Ottie sat on the front porch, holding a paper fan decorated with pale cherry blossoms in one hand and a tall glass of lemonade in the other. He invited Caleb to join him on the porch. Caleb took a seat, the dead rabbits on the porch between them like an offering.

He tried to think of a way to raise Gabriel's request with his boss. Ottie not only paid Caleb; he also owned his apartment in town, deducting the rent directly from his check. He let him use one of the farm trucks to get around and always found ways to keep him on the payroll, even during slow months. Ottie wasn't cheap, but Caleb doubted he would go for Gabriel's proposal.

Near the front fence, a juvenile jackrabbit lay with his hind legs splayed out in the shade of a wild rose bush. The old splintered boards of the porch creaked as Ottie leaned forward and shook his fan at the rabbit. "I thought you were taking care of those varmints!"

"I am, but it'll take time." Caleb removed his cap and fanned his face with the bill. "Besides we haven't seen any downturn in the field's production. They ain't really hurting anything and their population will crash soon enough."

"Once they've eaten all my melons and collapsed my house with their tunnels, you mean."

Caleb pictured the upstairs level with the yard. He and Ottie would be sitting on the porch underground, surrounded by cool dirt and the beady glowing eyes of hundreds of rabbits. "You got to admit times have been good, Ottie. The rabbits are a sure sign of that."

"I can't deny we've been in the Lord's fat little pocket the last few seasons." Ottie leaned back in his chair. "Just promise me you won't let them take over this place."

Caleb nodded.

"I need to talk to you about Gabriel."

Ottie gave him a cock-eyed look, as if to say *Who?* Caleb described Gabriel until he was certain Ottie knew which field hand he meant.

"What about him?" Ottie poured Caleb a glass of lemonade from the pitcher that sat between them.

Caleb took a slow drink. It was sour, with a bare hint of sugar, and caught in his dry throat. "He just enrolled over at Blue Mountain, wants to go to law school."

"Figures. He's always trying to talk his way out of something." Ottie batted a fly from his face and wiped his brow. "What's his status?"

"I think he was born in Yakima."

"But you don't know."

Caleb shook his head. "He needs some extra cash to cover expenses." A dust devil kicked up near the edge of the yard and scared the young rabbit back into his burrow.

Ottie sighed. "Look, I'm already paying for my own daughter to go to school. Lord knows I can't afford two loans." He rose, picked up the gunnysack of rabbits and turned toward the front door. He patted Caleb on the shoulder as he passed.

As Ottie reached the house, Caleb stood. "He's a good kid. Works hard, helps communicate with the other men."

"If he ever got a degree, he'd talk those men into suing me over conditions."

"He'd pay you back. He's a sound investment, worth the risk."

"Like you?" Ottie stood with his hand on the doorknob.

"With a better return."

Ottie turned and considered Caleb. His face was scrunched as though he were sucking on a lemon wedge. "I'll think about it," he said and he walked into the house. Alone on the porch, Caleb wasn't sure what to make of the old man's abrupt response. Was Ottie really considering the loan? Or was he just avoiding saying no?

Caleb left the porch and headed for the shed. Sheltered and shaded by a row of poplars, the shed remained cool, even during the heat of the day. He felt light headed as he entered the single room and pulled the chain for the overhead lamp. He took a quick inventory of the farm's supply of pesticide and fertilizer, and checked the container of rabbit corpses. The bin was partially full; he could wait another day or so to burn the bodies. The smell emitted when he lifted the lid didn't help his head. As he worked, Caleb wondered if he should tell Gabriel about his conversation with Ottie, or wait for more definite news.

He remembered coming to the house after his mother's first trip to the clinic. It was a cool fall evening but still they sat on the porch. Lauren had commandeered the kitchen table and covered it with vocabulary flashcards and study guides for the PSAT. Caleb didn't outright ask Ottie for a loan, but he assumed the request was clear when he mentioned scrapping his plans for trade school. Ottie smiled and patted him on the knee, told him not to worry about money. Then he offered Caleb a full-time job on the place. It seemed unlikely that Ottie would actually come through with a loan for Gabriel.

Caleb walked up the service road and approached the stand, still unsure whether to tell Gabriel anything. He stopped as he cleared the parking arrows, where the stand could be clearly viewed from across the yard. He watched Lauren and Gabriel, still snug behind the counter together, despite the stand's size and the day's heat. He saw their short laughs, controlled smiles and diverted glances. He wondered what Ottie would say if he saw them. Lauren placed a hand on Gabriel's shoulder and let the unspoiled skin of her palm linger there. Caleb's shoulders tightened.

"Lauren," he called out, "you mind letting Gabriel get back to work?" He was surprised by the rough edge to his voice. She rolled her eyes and rubbed Gabriel's shoulder before rising from the cooler. Gabriel blushed and greeted a customer. Lauren didn't look at Caleb. She passed him, headed for the house.

Caleb remained in the stand's doorway studying Gabriel. He knocked on a melon, then balanced it in his hands, before assuring the customer that it was ripe. Gabriel smiled, counted out change. Once the customer departed, he turned toward Caleb, but kept the smile fixed in place.

"I'm sorry," he said. "Lauren didn't want me to get bored out here in the stand. She offered to keep me company." He blushed again and looked out toward the parking lot for a moment. "It's all my fault and it won't happen again."

"I doubt I have to tell you what'd happen if Ottie saw it."

Gabriel diverted his glance to the counter. Caleb felt an unfamiliar pleasure in the fear he sensed in the kid.

"Did you talk to *Señor* Ottie?"

Caleb had anticipated Ottie's questions about Gabriel's status, the frugal sentiments. He would say no loan and that would be the end of it. But instead the old man was up there in the house, considering giving this kid the chance to get out. "No," he said. "I haven't talked to him about it yet."

Gabriel smiled and nodded. Another customer walked up to the wooden tiers. Caleb left the stand and went to check on the rest of the crew. They'd made it halfway across the northwest patch. He threw a set of keys to Ernesto and told them to spend the rest of day boxing melons for the morning truck in the shade of the barn. Then Caleb checked the pressure gauge and started watering the patch. The irrigation towers came to life, spreading a cool mist over the vines and dry soil. He shook his head at the wasteful method. Most of the water evaporated before it ever touched the ground.

Caleb walked back up the gravel driveway and knocked on the warped farmhouse door. Lauren greeted him with the same indifferent stare. She'd been infatuated with him as a girl, had constantly tried to catch his eye, once she got over her shyness. But girlish infatuations weren't meant for tired field hands. He wondered if she reserved those looks for Gabriel now or spread them out liberally. "I need to talk to your dad."

Lauren opened the screen and gestured with her head toward the living room, where Ottie sat in a floral overstuffed chair. He was flipping through the paper. A fan oscillated in the corner, near where the water cooler stood. Ottie wouldn't expose his little girl to the area's toxic tap water.

"What is it now, Beanpole?" He settled on the sports page as Caleb entered the room.

Lauren plopped down in another overstuffed chair. Her tan legs dangled over the armrest as she leafed through a book.

"I need to talk to you about Gabriel." Caleb watched Lauren, checking to see if she perked up at his name. She didn't seem to react.

"I told you I'd think about it."

Caleb turned his full attention to Ottie. "I know, but there's a new development." He took a deep breath. "Something you need to know before you make your decision."

Caleb gestured for Ottie to return to the porch, where they could speak. Lauren watched as they walked away, then turned back to her book. But Caleb was sure she was listening to every word they said through the window screens.

"What's he doing in the stand?" Ottie asked, as soon as the door was closed behind them. "It's not good for business. The customers won't trust him."

Caleb could hear some soccer mom from Bend lecturing Gabriel about properly selecting and handling quality fruit, even though the kid spent his days picking that produce. He would like to take these people out to the fields. Show them the hands that handled their food beneath the blistering sun. But Caleb knew Gabriel would say nothing.

"Gabriel in the stand is bad for business, but not because of the customers."

"What do you mean?"

"I just watched him make a sale. He was great with the customer, but pocketed the cash." Caleb was surprised how easily the lie slipped from his mouth. And wondered if it had been his intention all along.

Ottie shook his head. "You take care of the rabbits and the men. I'll take care of the problem." He reentered the house and closed the door behind him.

Caleb walked back down the driveway and positioned himself near the edge of the patch. He watched as Lauren walked to the stand, her eyes on the path before her. Gabriel would be next, headed for the house. Would he know what was coming? Would Lauren warn him? He turned and stared across the field.

Caleb avoided the stand and his crew for the rest of the day. He worked on equipment that wasn't in need of repair and checked the outer irrigation system for leaks. Like a rabbit when the tiller roars by, Caleb stayed on the edge of the fields and waited.

The stand was open, deserted, when he finally walked up the service road that evening. He turned off the fan but left the plywood shutters open. As he locked the door, crickets began to sing their night songs outside, clicking with the steady hum of the cars on the highway. Caleb wished he were in one of those cars, heading to Portland. He could leave these dusty patches behind and never look back. Make Ottie deal with day-to-day operations. See how Lauren liked the undivided attention of the field hands with no one to keep them on task. Forget the whole damn thing.

As he walked back toward his truck, scuffing his boots along the gravel path, a rabbit scurried out of the patch on his right. Caleb paused to examine the plant where the rabbit had emerged. The plant was void of interior leaves and blooms. Most of the vines had been broken off, their immature fruit spoiled. A melon, no bigger than his fist, rolled out onto the path, large bites gnawed into its rind. He picked up the ruined melon and looked out into the patch. The rabbit hadn't gone far. Sitting patiently, he was waiting for Caleb to leave.

Caleb tossed the half-gnawed melon toward the rabbit. The rabbit took one good hop, and then rose up on his haunches to examine Caleb. Now the rabbit was mocking him. Caleb charged toward the trespasser. The rabbit stood his ground for a moment before bolting for the edge of the patch. He zigged and zagged through the rows in an attempt to lose his pursuer. Caleb picked his way more cautiously through the vines, avoiding the melons. But he was determined to run the rabbit off. The jack reached the fence that was meant to keep rabbits out of the patch, and hit the wire with a loud thwack.

Caleb approached the fence, expecting to see the rabbit still running into the distance. The sun had begun to set, but the heat from the day remained, barely dissipated over the exposed field. His skin was sticky with sweat that plastered his clothes to him. Caleb leaned into the fence and panted. Then he noticed the jack, trapped under the wire. The front legs were through the gap, but the haunches had been too wide to slip through the opening. The rabbit thrashed at the base of the fence, staring at Caleb, eyes bright with panic.

Back toward Ottie's house, Caleb heard the back door screech open. Roscoe and Buckeye, the family's old hounds, yelped and howled, released to patrol the property. Caleb knew the rabbit wouldn't back out of the wire as long as he stood there; the jack's instinct told him to push forward.

Caleb rubbed the back of his neck and wished he knew someone with soft hands he could ask for a massage. Deep in his stomach Caleb felt a knot rise and twist. He knelt down near the rabbit as it trembled and kicked against the wire. For a moment, he considered pulling the wire apart, helping the jack to wriggle free. But he felt he'd done enough. Caleb rose, turned his back and walked to his truck.

Killdeer

The phone began vibrating in Drew's pocket at exactly 12:30, thirty minutes before last call. Parole officers never called this late, not even the anal ones. And he'd just finished swing at the mill, so he knew it wasn't the boss.

He didn't care to know who was calling just before closing time. Drew was more interested in eating something and getting some sleep. He monitored the pair of eggs frying on the stove. Drew liked his eggs thoroughly cooked, not runny in the slightest. He remembered how Mary Catherine would crinkle her nose as he made breakfast: "You're ruining them," she'd say. The yolks burst and spread quickly, covering the plate with milky liquid like a mudslide after the first strong rain, whenever she fixed them. His hand hovered over the pan, spatula at the ready.

The muffled buzz of the phone mingled with the low hum of the refrigerator and the pop of the eggs in the grease. Then the phone stopped vibrating and went to voicemail. The eggs were left to harmonize with the refrigerator. No singular pulse jarred his pocket, so no message.

The yolks turned a dull yellow, Drew flipped his eggs and put a piece of bread in the toaster. Again, the phone began to vibrate against his thigh. He pulled it from his pocket and stabbed the ignore button. The phone went still in his palm. Again, the caller left no message. He checked that the missed call was the same unknown number and stuffed the phone back in his pocket.

The bread sprang back into view, slightly burned. Drew slathered some blackberry jam on the toast, then slid the eggs from the pan, grease included, onto a small plate. He stood at the counter to eat. As he cut the first bite with a fork, the phone renewed its efforts to draw his attention away from food and sleep.

"Jesus," he mumbled as he retrieved the phone. He answered this time, afraid the constant calls would burn through his pre-paid minutes. "Yeah?"

"Drew, that you?" Tanner asked. "Look man, I need a ride."

"Where are you?" From the background murmur of voices and music, and the slur in Tanner's voice, he correctly guessed the answer.

"Sunset. You remember the place?"

Drew remembered the Sunset Tavern. It was directly across the parking lot from the Value Clean Laundromat where Tanner's sister worked. Mary Catherine drove them around most of the time back then, since she consistently had a valid license. While they waited for her, they self-medicated in her mini-van or drank and shot pool inside the Sunset.

In those days, they worked seasonally on the wildfire suppression crews. The job seemed ideal to Drew. You worked hard from late spring until the first heavy rains of fall and it paid enough to keep you in heroin for the rest of the year. Still, it was strange to have his livelihood dependent on destruction, natural or otherwise. He remembered that during one particularly slow season, Mary Catherine had offered to start a fire, just so they could get some work in. "Nothing big." She'd smiled at him. "Just a little grass fire along some ditch." Crew work was dirty and dangerous, but it was a damn sight better than pulling the green chain at the mill or setting chokers. At least that's what Drew told himself. But the fire chief didn't take convicted felons or known junkies.

"Yeah, I'll be there in fifteen. Meet me outside."

Tanner hung up without another word. Funny, he hadn't seen his old friend since the night Mary Catherine had him arrested. But her brother acted just like it was old times.

Drew covered the plate in foil and put it in the refrigerator. He'd heat it back up when he got home. He pulled on his boots and a quilted flannel jacket lined with fake sheep's wool. The sleeves were worn through at the elbows. Drew clasped the red Seven Feathers Casino poker chip that topped his keychain and moved to the door.

Outside, a resilient November snowstorm continued its attempt to bury the Umpqua Basin. The rest of Roseburg, sound asleep, would wake to a surprise. The wind blew steadily and two inches had already accumulated. Drew wondered how badly the city would be crippled by the storm. Roseburg, like many cities in the Pacific Northwest, was ill-prepared for winter. The problem was the rarity of real snow. It would be stupid to invest in a fleet of plows and a stockpile of salt. Lord knows, Douglas County didn't have a lot of extra money to spend.

Even though he'd just come home from the mill, his mustard-yellow Datsun pickup was reluctant to start in the cold. He brushed the snow from the windshield with his sleeve. In the cab, Drew cranked the key hard to the right. The truck clicked and squealed until it finally relented, turning over slowly three times, then sputtering to life.

Drew turned right onto Winchester Street and merged onto old Highway 99. There was no traffic. The snow sat in a loose layer over the pavement. He felt the Datsun shudder and shake with each minor adjustment of speed or turn of the wheel. At the first traffic light, the old truck skidded to a stop. Its nose protruded just beyond the outer limits of the crosswalk.

Even stationary, the snow slanting through the headlights like falling stars gave the illusion of motion to the Datsun. When the light changed, Drew pressed the accelerator and fishtailed through the intersection. After a block, he finally steadied the truck in its lane. He felt relieved that the road was empty.

After the truck repeated this performance at the next red light, Drew pulled off in the Safeway parking lot. From behind the seat, he grabbed a collapsible shovel and piled snow into the bed for ballast. Finished, he wiped his brow and stared at the sky as he coughed hard from exertion.

Overhead, the snowflakes dashed in and out of the yellow glow of the street lamps, as if trying to draw his attention away from the truck. Drew remembered waiting for the school bus in fourth grade. A killdeer harassed him every morning that spring. The tawny bird had laid her eggs on the ground somewhere nearby, probably in the gravelly ditch. A killdeer will fuss and act as if its wing is broken to lure predators away from its nest. The prospect of an easily captured bird was more appealing than a mouthful of small speckled eggs.

"The killdeer tries to trick you into giving up something good. Leads you off in the wrong direction," his father told him. "Then just when you think she's yours, bam! She's gone." The old man always illustrated this last point by cupping his hands into a fake balloon, then crushing it into invisible powder.

Drew never saw the nest and didn't care where it was hidden. Still, the killdeer was insistent that he not stand at the end of the long gravel driveway. *Follow me,* she urged, as she dragged her wing back and forth in the dust. At first, he found the display interesting, but as the days wore on and the killdeer failed to relent, Drew found her cries and dramatics annoying. Still, his father insisted, "It's not her fault. It's her nature. You can't blame a killdeer for being a killdeer, son."

With the added weight, the truck was more balanced. The back tires gripped the road and the Datsun stopped fishtailing. Drew continued north on Old 99 toward Winchester, the road turning darker as the houses and businesses thinned out.

The Sunset Tavern hadn't changed since he'd last been there, four years prior. The exterior was still painted teal with orange trim, capped with a rusted metal roof. There was no sign of Tanner. The parking lot was virtually empty; in this weather, most of the patrons hadn't waited for last call.

As he sat in the cab and waited for Tanner to emerge from the bar, Drew thought about his own plans for the day. First, get some sleep, then wake in the afternoon, shower and shave, and eat a TV dinner. Then head back to the mill in Riddle for another shift, if the snow didn't close the road.

In his rearview mirror, Drew could make out the faint glow from the Value Clean's neon sign. He wondered if Mary Catherine still worked there. He hoped not. The last time Drew had seen Mary Catherine was at his parole hearing. He'd just completed rehab and was being released to work crew. Visibly pregnant and crying, Mary Catherine begged the judge not to impose the mandatory restraining order on him. Even without the order, Drew knew he wouldn't see her again. But he remained silent as she went on.

Mary Catherine had called the sheriff immediately after he slapped her hard across the face. They were at the peak of their latest argument about nothing. The slap echoed through their cramped apartment like dry thunder, where no rain falls to break the tension. The argument stopped. She looked back at him, blood on her mouth, no words. Mary Catherine moved with purpose to the phone on the counter. And Drew made no attempt to stop her. Rather, he went to the living room, sat on the couch, stretched his neck as he rubbed the back of his head, and waited.

She regretted the call even before the police arrived. "Why don't you go?" she'd said. "You can't be here when they get here."

But Drew didn't move at first. He continued to wait for the sheriff, even as her suggestions became more urgent and pleading. At the last moment he fled, squeezing through the narrow bathroom window, then staggering down the street. This was more from an instinct that he had to try, not thinking he'd actually get away. He didn't make it even half a block.

Of course, the deputy had to be Junior Billingsley, the punk who'd tormented him throughout high school. Junior tackled him hard on the sidewalk, stabbing his knee into Drew's back. "Just like old times in PE, asshole." And he'd chuckled as he cuffed him extra tight.

Like idiots, Drew and Mary Catherine had agreed to Junior's demand to search the apartment. He found Drew's stash in his closet, and a scale and sandwich bags in the kitchen. Drew was charged with domestic violence, resisting arrest, and possession of heroin with intent to distribute.

Mary Catherine didn't know his stash was inside, and neither of them knew she was pregnant. "He didn't mean to hurt me," she told the court. "And I don't want to lose him. I just wanted to scare him, is all."

The judge cut her off. He lectured her about Drew's history of violence, his prior assault with a weapon conviction. When she explained that that was just a bar fight, one swipe with a dull pocketknife, she might as well have held up an **ENABLER** sign. The judge then turned to Drew and made it clear that the restraining order was part of his parole, and if violated, he would go to jail.

Still no sign of Tanner. Drew reluctantly killed the Datsun's engine. He hadn't been inside the Sunset since his release. It wasn't the sort of place his PO generally encouraged him to hang around.

Inside the dimly lit bar, the air was warm and stale. In some ways, the conditions weren't that different from the mill, just with a more open layout. Both places had perpetual low lights and sour air, no matter the time of day or season. Both had sawdust on the floor. And both were usually filled with men complaining about their bills and their wives at home. Like the outside, the tavern's interior was unchanged. Drew remembered the hours he and Tanner had wasted shooting pool, listening to old loggers longing for the State of Jefferson, while across the parking lot Mary Catherine folded sheets and wrangled lost socks.

It wasn't hard to spot Tanner. He slouched over the bar, an open Rainier stubby in front of him.

Drew tapped Tanner on the shoulder. "You were supposed to meet me outside."

"In this weather?" He swiveled on the stool to face Drew. "Piss off."

"Ready?"

"What's the hurry?" he asked. "Sit down. Let me buy you a drink, brother." Tanner gestured for the bartender, who was cleaning glasses at the other end of the bar.

Drew waved him off. Outside of a small group in a booth across the room, there wasn't anyone to distract the bartender from serving them. Still, he seemed content to continue to clean the glasses.

"Thought you needed a ride?"

Tanner turned back toward the bar. "I do," he said. "But it ain't last call."

"Let's go." Drew grabbed Tanner's elbow and lifted his old friend off the stool.

Tanner jerked away and staggered into the bar. He knocked the Rainier over, but managed to put the seat between them. "Look what you made me do," he said.

"There a problem?" asked the bartender, suddenly interested, towel in hand.

"Nah," said Tanner. "My friend here just gets a little grabby when he's had a drink. Ain't that right, Drew?"

Drew felt his fist clench and release. He couldn't tell if Tanner was trying to make some point about their past or just making a joke at his expense. "Sorry," he said. "We were just leaving."

The bartender nodded toward the door and wiped up the spilled beer. Tanner closed his tab. The two men left the almost-empty tavern.

Back in the Datsun, the engine had cooled and Drew again had to crank the key to get the motor to turn over. "You still live in Mill-Pine?" he asked as they headed back to Roseburg.

Tanner sank into the seat, shaking his head. "Glide. You'd know that if you spent any time with your son."

Glide was more of a drive than he'd bargained for in these conditions, especially with the sort of mood Tanner was in. His passenger let out a long belch as he continued to adjust himself in the narrow seat.

"When'd you move?"

"After Mary Catherine got a job tending bar at the Narrows," he said. "We rent a little house behind the lounge."

Drew wondered why Tanner still hung out at the Sunset if he lived behind a bar. "She ever go back to school?" He kept his eye on the road but in the periphery he could make out Tanner cocking his head.

"School?" Tanner made a noise that sounded like a cough, a laugh, or some combination of the two. "Yeah, I guess you could say she did. Never seems to stick with it, though." He dug in his pockets and pulled out a pack of cigarettes. "Got a light?"

Drew shook his head. "Don't smoke that in here."

Tanner searched his pockets and finally produced a matchbook. "It ain't gonna hurt nothing," he said and lit up. Smoke began to fill the cab.

"Why didn't it stick?"

"What?"

"School," Drew said. "Why didn't Mary Catherine stick with it?"

"Can't afford it. Too busy looking for someone to be a father to your son. Or maybe she's just too dumb." He made the noise again. "Take your pick."

At the light, Drew reached across the cab and cracked the passenger window. "At least roll down the window."

"Fuck you, it's cold." Tanner rolled the window back up.

Drew cracked his own window. It would be a lot colder if

I left your ass on the sidewalk, he wanted to say, but thought better of it. "You still working wildfire season?"

"Nah, ain't got the knees for it anymore. I'm self-employed these days."

"What's that supposed to mean?"

"Well, let's just say your arrest gave me an idea." Tanner slumped forward and held his hands near the heater. "I'm always looking for new customers, if you're ever in need."

"You know I'm sober," he said. "It's bad enough you making me pull you outta that bar."

"You think you're better than me, just cause your sleeves are rolled down. But I didn't make you do anything you didn't want to. Never have. You forget, I know you. You liked this shit more than I ever did."

Drew felt the old familiar pulse in his veins, the empty longing that never really went away. He'd been clean for three years, none of which were easy. There were plenty of days after work that he would have liked nothing more than to shoot up. He missed the calm, numb feeling that used to wash over him after the initial sting of the needle.

Tanner reached into his coat's interior pocket. "My product's high quality, nearly medical grade." He took an Altoids tin from his pocket and placed it on the seat between them. "Better than that junk you used to score."

Drew tried to keep his eyes on the road. The beams of the Datsun's headlights swarmed with falling snow. "Put that shit away. You know I can't."

"Why? Cause the court told you not to? Is that why you never call my sister? Why you've never even seen your son?"

While the restraining order didn't apply to Drew's son, it was impossible to see him in Mary Catherine's presence. He couldn't afford supervised visits and he didn't know anyone qualified who would do it for free. Drew's monthly paycheck went to child support, rent, and the Datsun. He lived on food stamps, gas vouchers, and a pre-paid government-issued phone. There was nothing to spare. Or at least that's what he told himself.

"I could go to prison," he said. "I'm no good to either of them locked up."

"You're in prison now."

"You don't know what you're talking about."

"And you don't have a clue what this is about."

Drew turned to face Tanner, forgetting the road and the snow. "Then why don't you tell me what the fuck this is all about?"

"Your sobriety is a delusion," Tanner said. "You abandoned us."

The Datsun swayed slightly, pushed by the winter wind. Drew firmly gripped the steering wheel and tried to keep the truck steady. Not that it mattered if he drifted into the other empty lanes.

"Abandoned?"

"You don't have to see the assholes Mary Catherine brings home, considers at the bar. Watch her cry her eyes out with each false pregnancy scare, praying for another miscarriage. Or try to explain to your son why his father doesn't even call."

"I support them." Drew returned his attention to the road.

"And we feel blessed by the checks you graciously send on the state's behalf," Tanner sneered. "But the kid needs a father."

"Good thing he's got his dealer uncle around to fill that void."

"Fuck you. I'm just doing what you never had the balls to do. I take care of my family," Tanner said.

Drew made the hard left onto Diamond Lake Boulevard toward Glide too fast. The truck skidded through the turn, jostling both men.

"Jesus!" Tanner cried. "Watch what you're doing."

But as the truck straightened out, Drew accelerated. He wanted this night to be over. He wanted Tanner and the heroin out of his truck. Most of all, Drew wanted to get some sleep.

As the Datsun approached the Winchester intersection, a stalled Honda Civic came into view. The hatchback was stuck in the middle of the left lane.

"Watch out." Tanner braced himself on the doorframe.

Drew turned the wheel hard right and went into a slide. The truck missed the Civic, but skidded off the road onto the strip of grass and trees that buffered the library's parking lot from the street. He hit the salmon sculpture head on, stopping just shy of the first barren tree. Drew could already feel the burn from the seatbelt forming across his collarbone. Tanner groaned and rubbed a bloody lip. The painted salmon, once poised to rise from the Umpqua's rapids, now rested on the Datsun's hood. The pink flesh stood out in stark contrast with the falling snow.

The engine was dead. Drew turned the key but was met with silence. "Shit." He tried again. Still no response. He'd have to retrieve the truck in the daylight. Luckily it wasn't blocking the road, so it shouldn't be towed immediately. Drew got out, slamming the driver's door hard behind him.

He walked out into the street and around the Civic. Judging by the amount of snow piled on the car, it had been sitting there for at least the last half hour. The tracks leading to it had already begun to fill with fresher snow. Drew peered through the windows. No one was inside. With no obvious damage to the car, he was at a loss for why it had been abandoned there. Satisfied that no one was stranded, he walked back toward the Datsun.

On the corner, Tanner moaned as he stretched his back and shoulders. "Now what?"

"Your mom still live in Mill-Pine?"

Tanner nodded.

"Better start walking."

"In this?"

Drew shrugged. "We ain't going anywhere in the Datsun." He turned to leave his old friend and the truck on the corner, but he paused at the intersection, not sure why he was waiting for the light. Then Drew swung around and returned to the cab. Tanner's tin of heroin was still on the seat. For a moment, he considered slipping it into his jacket. After all, Tanner had offered it freely; he couldn't complain. And how good a fix would feel before he collapsed into his warm bed. Drew weighed the tin in his palm.

He emerged from the cab and tossed the tin to Tanner: "Be sure to take this with you."

Drew locked the truck and started for home again.

"This doesn't change anything," Tanner called after him. "You're not a father, you ain't responsible, and you won't be able to stay clean forever." He held the tin up and waved it back and forth above his head. "You ain't better than me. You need this shit."

And the killdeer's wing is really broken, Drew thought.

As Drew crossed Diamond Lake Boulevard to walk the four blocks to his apartment, Tanner continued to shout at him about all the things he wasn't. Drew never turned back to face the scene. The last discernible thing he heard Tanner scream over the wind was "You're nothing, just like the rest of us. Just too fuckin' stuck up to see it."

Back at his place he was too tired to eat. Drew decided to head straight to bed. He removed his boots and coat, dropped them on the living room floor, and headed upstairs in his stocking feet. He could eat and clean up after he got some sleep.

Drew sat on his bed and watched the snow continue to fall through his grimy window. The room stayed cold, despite the sputtering electric wall heater. In the distance, he could see downtown Roseburg, nestled in the dip between hills and the river. The glow of street lamps and traffic lights illuminated the snow against an otherwise dark sky.

He wondered how far Tanner had made it in the storm. Had he managed to convince anyone else to drive him to Glide? Did he offer the tin in gratitude? Drew shifted his gaze east toward Glide, but with fewer lights he was met with darkness and his own opaque reflection in the window. Was Mary Catherine still up? Or did she close up the bar and go to bed, accustomed to the men in her life being absent? Drew imagined she sat outside their son's room and listened to him sleep.

He pulled the phone from his pocket and flipped it open. Through muscle memory, he dialed Mary Catherine's number, or at least the last one he knew. Finished, his thumb hovered above the *send* button. He wanted to call, just to tell her that Tanner should be on his way to Grandma Nancy's. That he knew about the other guys. That he'd pay her tuition if he could. But mostly he wanted to ask about his son and tell her he was sorry. And why shouldn't he call? Yes, Drew knew it would be in direct violation of his parole, but after visiting the bar, picking up a known user and nearly wrecking his truck he figured he already had plenty to explain to his PO. What was one more thing?

On the hills beyond the city, Drew saw the outlines of houses, some with Christmas lights already lining their eaves. The whole scene outside his window looked unreal, too tranquil and pristine. No, Drew thought, it looked more like a miniature model than a real town. The heater continued to sputter; the coils glowed orange in the wall. He lay back on the bed, exhausted but unable to sleep. The phone was still cradled in his hand, his thumb suspended over the *send* button.

A Certain Kind of Luck

That summer, Jake started sleeping with a blue ice pack pressed against his back. Lena wouldn't sleep unless she was held, and heat poured off her like a dryer vent. Jake had a low tolerance for heat; even lying near Karen in bed caused him to perspire. With the addition of the baby, a natural space heater cradled against his chest, the ice pack was a necessity.

Holding the baby at night was his second job now. Initially, Karen had insisted on doing all of the night comforting herself. Jake was still working full time and freelancing in the evening, to earn extra cash to replace his wife's income. But after three months without sleep, Karen made it clear she needed his help. So after dinner he would do a little work in his office, make sure he had fully emptied his bladder, then begin the sleep march.

Most nights, simply holding Lena wasn't enough to put her to sleep. First, she had to be walked with a bouncing gait, near the dim light of the western windows. Jake stroked her hair and cooed in her ear, as he described the different objects they bounced past in a singsong voice. Lena could get heavy as a bag of rice when carried continuously for three hours, for even when she wasn't ready to sleep she wanted to be held and carried. Unable to move efficiently on her own, she relied on her parents to help her observe. Eventually, the steady rhythm of his strides and words lulled her to sleep.

Jake would move toward the kitchen, still bouncing, and slowly open the freezer door. He would shift her limp weight to one arm and retrieve the blue ice with his free hand. The freezer door, hopefully, would shut gently, so no one was disturbed by the sound. Then he wrapped the ice in one of the dishtowels, the long ones with the word "TEA" woven in tan block letters across one end.

On most nights, the ritual would end there. Despite her potent heat production, his daughter was a sound sleeper once she went down. She was undisturbed by night sounds or the discomfort of others. Provided contact with her parents was never broken, Lena would sleep through the night. And so would Jake, the baby sandwiched between his arm and Karen and an ice pack wedged against his back.

But on that particular August night, after the Portland-Vancouver area had smoldered through a week of triple digit temperatures, no amount of cooing and bouncing would put Lena to sleep. Jake put her in the crib, thinking that perhaps she had reached her limit in the heat as well. Besides, Karen had read that they should start trying to encourage her to self-sooth. She seemed stunned as he laid her down, dimmed the lights and turned the ceiling fan on low. Before she could move, he bolted from the nursery, leaving the door cracked.

In the living room, Jake and Karen sat on opposite ends of the couch and listened while Lena screamed. They had placed a box fan on high in the patio door, with a block of ice in front of it and a damp towel draped across the back, a makeshift air conditioner. The air outside stayed still. The only noises in the house were the roar of the box fan and their daughter's plaintive cries.

Fifteen minutes into the standoff, Karen sighed and stood up. She began to walk toward the nursery.

He grabbed her arm. "Where do you think you're going?"

"I can't stand to listen to her any longer," she said.

"But the book said we're supposed to let her cry it out."

"The author of that book probably never had children." She tugged her arm free of his grasp. "Besides you gave up on her too fast, didn't give her a chance to transition."

"Now just a minute." Jake got to his feet and maneuvered himself between her and the hallway. His head throbbed. His whole body felt hot and uncomfortable. "The car used to put her to sleep." Their midsized Toyota sedan offered both continuous motion and actual air conditioning. "I'll take her for a ride," he said. "You get some sleep."

Not much had changed in the nursery, except Lena stood propped on the crib rail. No wonder she hadn't fallen asleep, standing with her legs braced. Jake marveled that she hadn't flipped herself out in desperation. Lena's face was crimson from the heat, streaked with tears. On the floor was her stuffed turtle, Tait, hurled from the crib as if to say: *You would make me sleep without Tait*? She glared up at him and continued to wail, unwilling to forgive his betrayal.

Jake grabbed the diaper bag and Tait before retrieving Lena. Back in the living room, he laid her back in the car seat. He didn't think she had a higher volume, but securing the straps seemed to kick her screaming up a notch. Lena squirmed and reached toward her parents' bedroom, as though she sensed that Karen was hiding there. The straps adjusted, Jake grabbed his keys, shouldered the bag, picked up the car seat and headed for the garage, thankful he had parked inside. At least he wouldn't subject the neighborhood to his daughter's unfiltered screams.

After Lena was secured atop her car seat's base, Jake adjusted the AC and tried to direct the streams of cool air back to her. The car's interior was stuffy but already seemed cooler than the house. He watched her strain against the straps and sob in the mirror attached to the headrest of the back seat. She returned his gaze with trembling lips and he averted his eyes. He pointed the car toward the onramp for I-5 North, just a few blocks from the house. *Smooth continuous motion,* he thought. *Do the circuit between Hazel Dell and Kalama and she'll fall asleep.*

Just past the I-205 interchange, they passed the county fairgrounds. The Ferris wheels and other carnival rides lit up the sky with garish spirals of neon light. He remembered the first time he'd brought Karen down from Seattle shortly after they were married. They had gone to the fair. The highlight was milkshakes from the Dairy Princess booth, the flavor somehow enhanced by the fresh smell of cow shit from the adjacent barn.

Karen had been poised and dignified throughout a day full of unsubtle inquiries from his mother about when she could expect a full complement of grandchildren. She only flinched when Jake suggested riding the Ferris wheel. Despite a slight fear of heights, Karen had agreed, provided Jake didn't rock the carriage. Her soft, small and quivering hand clutched his as their seats reached the top. Whenever the carriage descended she loosened her grip, pulled her hand completely away for a moment, and rested her head on his shoulder.

Jake was careful to make every turn and change of speed as fluid as possible. He wondered if babies became velocitized. He remembered the warning in driver's-ed, one of the many dangers of high-speed freeway driving. He had no memory of losing the sensation of speed before driving himself. Maybe that was the danger, you didn't notice.

He checked the mirror relay. Silent tears streamed down Lena's face as her eyes darted about the car. Her little hands punched the air, clenched in red fists. Jake thought of Karen at home and her nights of tears and frustration. Karen felt guilty about Lena's needy sleep habits, and her inability to console her. One sleep-deprived morning, after the baby took four hours to put down, she'd confessed between sobs that she resented their daughter. *What kind of mother feels that way?* she'd screamed, before collapsing into a seat.

The next night Jake took over the graveyard shift, as they half-jokingly called the long walk for sleep. And things got better for a while, although Karen still felt depressed and sick with guilt. Although he realized her conflict, Jake had initially taken up the task with a secret joy. He was eager to do better than Karen, to prove he was a modern man who wasn't limited to the role of breadwinner. But as the weeks dragged into summer and the nightly ritual became more involved, that changed. Now he felt the urge to snap at Karen that he had to work in the morning. Pull yourself together and take care of your daughter. When it's all you have to do, how hard can it be? These thoughts simmered inside Jake, a sour, sick feeling in his stomach. He wondered if Karen was sitting up now, anxious about where they were. Or was she sound asleep?

At that hour the highway was mostly empty, with the exception of convoys of trucks eager to put miles behind them while traffic was thin. Outside, I-5 followed the curve of the Columbia River. Suddenly, Lena's protests and pleadings picked back up, as if her voice had returned from a smoke break. "Darling, please," he said. "There aren't any whales in that river, so no more wailing." But she didn't appreciate the pun, and continued to kick and cry.

The darker shadow of Mount Saint Helens rose to the east of the highway. In middle school, he'd taken field trips to the Ape Cave, disappointingly named for a Boy Scout troop, not Sasquatch. Below the collapsed dome, the Lahar had stretched out, desolate and dusty, a scarred strip of land left barren by the mudflows caused by the eruption. Jake had no memory of the mountain's nearly symmetrical peak; it had erupted before he was born. All he knew were stories of air thick with ash and pictures of a perfect white ball above the timberline. His great aunt Janis had owned a cabin on Spirit Lake and climbed the mountain every summer before the eruption. The cabin had been destroyed. The uninsured property was wiped away. Still, Janis never said a word about her personal or financial losses. And she only spoke fondly of the mountain.

North of Woodland, he decided to turn on the radio. OPB sputtered out of the speakers, the BBC News Service heavy with static. He hit the search button and found a smooth jazz station. But the hum of the engine, the vibration of the car, and the mellow music did little to soothe Lena.

Jake scratched his head and watched a freight train cut through the night. As a boy he'd been fascinated with the optical illusion that made it difficult to tell whether a train was moving or stationary, when viewed from a passing car. His mother had used trains as an opportunity to distract her children, challenging them to count all the boxcars. Unfortunately, that trick wouldn't work on Lena. The train also followed the river, but in the opposite direction from their car.

Jake clicked off the radio. As the train rumbled past, he noticed that a stillness had crept into the car. Lena had stopped crying. He glanced at her mirror-relayed image, and noticed that Tait lay helpless on his back, dropped on the seat next to her. She fidgeted, rubbed her eyes and blinked heavily. A few miles later, Jake could barely make out the smallest of snores over the engine noise.

But when he got to Kalama, he didn't turn around. With Lena asleep, he knew he should. There was no reason for him to drive aimlessly with his daughter in the back seat. He had little doubt Karen was still awake, waiting for them. The bed would seem empty to her without them. If he turned around now as he'd planned, there was still a chance to get a decent night's sleep before the 6:00 AM alarm.

Instead Jake continued north, toward Seattle. Or, he thought, maybe I'll cut west at Rochester and head for the Olympic Peninsula. He'd spent several summers with Janis hiking near Lake Quinault. There was a peace there, kneeling on the damp moss, concealed in a thicket of ferns. For months after those trips, his clothes retained the scent of cedar. He breathed deep, but the Toyota's interior only smelled of fake pine.

On his last hike with Janis, before Alzheimer's took her memory and she was forced into the sterile walls of the assisted living home in Olympia, they'd found the skeleton of an elk in a creek bed. It was August and the only sign of water in the ravine was the grass that grew up through the ribs. Jake examined the bones, picked clean by turkey vultures, while Janis prepared lunch.

Janis placed her hand on his shoulder. She held his sandwich in the other hand, balanced on a tin plate. They used a nearby log as a bench and a table, although they had to flick ants from their legs as they ate. Jake asked his great aunt what killed the elk.

"Hard to say," she said between huge bites of her lunch. She always ate with gusto on the trail. "But given the position of the bones with no evidence of trauma, I'd say he starved."

Jake had only eaten half his sandwich by the time she'd finished. He continued to stare at the bones, glaring white in a sunbeam. Janis patted his knee. She spoke plainly, like a narrator in a nature documentary, "When there isn't enough food, young bucks have to separate from their herds."

She stroked his hair back, bleached blonde by the sun. "They don't want to leave their families but they have to. It's their only shot at survival. Sometimes life just bears down on us, Jakey." Then she gestured around the ravine. "But could you ask for a better place to rest?" Janis laughed, and Jake laughed with her, as they enjoyed the good fortune of the bones. He finished the rest of his sandwich and they continued on their way toward Enchanted Valley, singing the Geoduck song, the chorus echoing off the cedar trunks.

Before Karen got pregnant, he'd planned a trip to Lake Quinault for their anniversary. His probationary period with the state was over, and they were both working again. But fetal Lena shifted their priorities, with future budget restrictions and house payments on their minds. The weekend away was postponed, then scrapped.

As if on cue, Lena whimpered from the back seat. Jake checked the mirror relay and saw her shift slightly as her eyes flickered open. She was barely awake, but enough to resist the notion of going back to sleep. Jake wondered if she was searching for Tait, still stranded on his back, or for the warm cocoon of her parents' bodies around her.

The last time he'd been out to Lake Quinault was his twenty-fifth birthday. Karen had surprised him with a room in the lodge. They were still living in Seattle and were just engaged the month before, and Jake hadn't lost his advertising job yet. The room was barebones, adorned only with a bed, small dresser and nightstand. The full bed was the smallest they'd occupied together since their dorm days.

It was early May and rained the entire weekend. But still they managed to get out for a hike. A laminated flier at the Petes Creek trailhead warned of the possible presence of cougars. Karen was concerned, but made the effort for him. She clutched his hand as they walked, asking after every crunch of gravel, drop of rain, or movement in the brush. When she confessed to Jake that she had a funny feeling about the trail, he finally relented and they headed back to the lodge.

On the way back from the trailhead, they stopped at the world's largest Sitka Spruce, located only a few feet off the road. Jake wondered if they cut down larger trees that grew in less convenient locations. Or did they bribe record keepers, to conceal the existence of those trees from visitors? The two of them spent the rest of the afternoon playing cribbage by the enormous stone fireplace. At dinner, a waiter told them that a biker had been mauled that afternoon on the trail they'd abandoned.

Lena's whimpers were becoming more frequent. Jake pulled off the freeway in search of a safe place to stop and check on his daughter. While idling at a stop light, he tapped the steering wheel, checked the mirror relay, and cooed to Lena.

The intersection was empty, except for a lone woman in a small hatchback directly behind them. At first Jake paid her little attention, until her movements in his rearview mirror became too distracting. She rubbed reddened eyes behind tortoise shell glasses. She worked hard not to disturb the placement of the glasses, even as she pushed harder into her sockets. At first, he wrote the action off as her own attempt to ward off sleep on the final stretch of her drive. Or maybe she had something in her eye. But she kept pawing at her eyes, even as the light changed and they both pulled through the intersection.

Worried about her ability to drive, he kept glancing back at her peculiar actions. As he pulled to another gradual stop at the next vacant intersection, he realized that she had been fighting to hold back tears. Now the woman removed her tortoise shell glasses and lost it. Her face elongated into a tight, grotesque grimace just before she buried it in her hands.

Jake sat in his car and felt helpless. What was she crying about? He looked at his daughter in the mirror, her own cheeks still showing the stains of tears. He thought of Karen at home and her recent nights of tears and frustration. Was she sleeping now or sitting up, crying, worried about where they were?

The light seemed like it would never change. The woman in the tortoise shell glasses continued to sob in his rearview mirror. He wondered if he should get out, ask her if she needed help. Or at least offer her a tissue. Tissues, something he had never kept in his car before Lena was born. But as Jake debated, the woman reached across her car and retrieved a tissue from the glove box. Slowly she seemed to be regaining control, although Jake could see that she was still upset, too distracted to drive.

She honked and gestured toward the intersection. The light had changed. The woman in the tortoise shell glasses turned left, while he continued straight through the intersection. Within seconds, she was out of his sight; there was nothing more he could do but wonder. Were they tears of despair, anger, or frustration? Had someone died? Was she driving away from trouble, or headed for it? Did her boyfriend abuse her, cheat on her with her best friend?

Jake told himself the reason for her tears shouldn't matter to him. Maybe there wasn't a reason. Still there was something unnerving about her silent sobs, her sadness perfectly contained within the car. He drove around the block and headed back toward the freeway. With no overpass, he had no choice but to continue north. Headed north again, a few cars and trucks continued to stream down I-5, unaware of the woman's tears. For all Jake knew, he was the only witness to her pain. He convinced himself that contacting her wouldn't have helped. But he couldn't shake the feeling that he was just another man who had failed her that night.

Lena's fussing, rekindled by the car horn, increased and Jake gently shushed her. He took a deep breath, realizing his chance to get Lena to sleep easily was gone. He remembered that Karen sang Lena little songs, lullabies she had learned at a *Mommy and Me* class. But he hadn't attended any of those classes. All the songs he knew weren't appropriate for babies. So Jake sang the only one he could think of:

Oh it takes a lot of pluck and a certain kind of luck
just to dig around the muck, just to find a geoduck.
And he doesn't have a front and he doesn't have a back.
He doesn't know Donald, and he doesn't go quack.

But it was no use. Lena continued to resist the sleep her little body so desperately wanted. Unwilling to return in failure, Jake pulled into a rest stop and picked up Tait. He jiggled him in Lena's face, before placing the turtle on her lap. But still she cried.

On the seat next to him, his phone began to vibrate, Karen's picture flashing across the screen. Jake pressed ignore call, clutched the steering wheel and pressed his forehead against the window. God damn it, he thought, I can't even think of one song to comfort my own daughter. He wondered if there were any rooms available at the Lake Quinault Lodge.

Jake killed the engine and got out of the car. He retrieved Lena from her car seat. Across the narrow strip of pavement, a handful of weary travelers milled about the free coffee stand. For a moment Lena stopped crying, perhaps shocked by the audience, to be out of the car, in the night air, or back in her father's arms. But it didn't last. So Jake cooed in her ear and began to pace about the rest area, back and forth, with a bouncing gait. He rubbed her back and in her ear he softly sang. His voice low and raspy:

Dig a duck, dig a duck, dig a geoduck.
Dig a duck, dig a geoduck, dig a duck a day---

After a few passes in the open air, when she realized he wasn't going to stop, Lena began to calm down. Once her body became limp, her weight pulling his arms toward the pavement, then he'd check the rest area map and find the nearest overpass. He'd text Karen before driving south. Let her know that Lena was asleep and they were on their way home. With any luck, Jake would be able to turn around before it was too late.

Beware of Darkness

Throughout the sales yard, grounded gargoyles kept a silent vigil. Ceramic Buddhas, unperturbed by the blustery skies, smiled fixed smiles. The concrete deer stood startled, poised to bolt, while lesser Greek gods, a bit mossy from repeated showers, reached toward Olympus. The cement lawn ornaments spiraled out from the central gazebo and soaked under the fall rain. There were no customers; the only movement in the yard was the steady flow of what was meant to suggest urine from a row of little resin boys, chubby and naked, each with one hand cocked on his hip and the other guiding the stream. They stood with bent knees and mischievous expressions below their wavy locks. The only sound beside the rain was Dale's hands, clicking the needles.

He sat hunched on the covered porch behind the garage storefront, a ball of navy blue yarn resting at his feet on the splintered boards. The slender needles looked out of place in his calloused hands. He had quit smoking twenty years ago, the first time Frances was pregnant, but still needed something to occupy his hands. Oddly, he found the replacement early on in knitting. And yet he still wasn't an accomplished knitter. After all these years, he could only make broad scarves, which he sold alongside the birdfeeders, seed, and other garden knickknacks in the shop.

Frances and Dale had started the home business five years ago, after the mill cut his hours. There was plenty of space they weren't using. They purchased the house early in their marriage. Frances had insisted they'd need a big place, lots of room for the kids to run around and play. But the only kids in the yard either came with their parents to look at the lawn gnomes, or they were naked and made of stone.

Today, a cold, stiff pain lingered in his fingers as he placed the needles on the bench. Dale scanned the yard, but tried not to linger on the ornaments. He'd never cared for the statues; he found their blank stares unnerving. They reminded him of the troll figurine that stood on his grandmother's mantel. The troll was a Cyclops, and the oversized eye was devoid of any expression. A tuft of coarse black hair adorned the end of his short tail. He stood upright, grinning, with a single tooth exposed beneath his bulbous nose, his gnarled fists holding the straps of his green overalls. Grandma Margie had brought the figure back from Norway, after one of her trips to discover the family's roots.

Margie told him how the *huldrefolk* came to life in darkness, then turned back to stone when touched with light. Most of them were ugly, like the troll, but some looked like regular people, except for a hidden tail or a misshapen ear. As a boy, Dale would take the figure to the top of his grandparents' staircase, close the door to the upper story and turn the lights out. As darkness settled in the stairwell, six-year-old Dale would flinch with anticipation. He tested his young courage, waiting on the stairs for a few seconds, before bolting back to the safety of the bright living room. Dale never saw the troll come to life, and wasn't sure he wanted to. Still, he repeated this experiment on every visit until his grandparents moved out of the old farmhouse. Their new ranch style home was well lit and offered few places to secretly test the troll. Gradually, as Dale entered adolescence, his interest in the figure waned.

Dale unfolded the morning newspaper and flipped through the first section. The cat killers dominated the front page again. Three local boys had been arrested several months back for shooting cats. For weeks, the teenagers had driven around the sparsely populated northern end of the county, using cats for target practice with their fathers' small caliber handguns. The sheriff estimated more than two dozen had been shot, before guilt got the better of one of the kids. He turned himself in and implicated the others.

The article featured their picture after the arraignment, slouched and chewing their lips, fiddling with ties they had probably last worn to homecoming, as they stood on the courthouse steps. Dale knew the guilt-stricken one, Kevin, and he lingered on his picture. Kevin was their only part-time employee. He helped move the statues and kept the gravel display yard weed free. Not officially fired, Kevin hadn't been back to work since his arrest. For the moment he was grounded, awaiting sentencing.

They were all seniors at Brush Prairie High School, good students, never in trouble. When the reporter asked why they had done it, Kevin said, *We weren't thinking, we were, like, just bored.* Dale realized that Jacob would have started at Brush Prairie Middle School this year, but he pushed the thought out of his head. The boys would be sentenced in the next few days.

Frances padded past him, on her way from house to store. She acknowledged her husband with a quick nod as she passed. Sputnik, their old tortoiseshell cat, followed her, daintily placing her paws on the wet sidewalk with each step. The cat ignored Dale, but gestured at the ball of yarn.

Dale dropped the paper by his leg. Frances was horrified when she'd first read about the mysterious cat slaughter. She had insisted they keep Sputnik inside until the criminals were found. The cat rarely went out after dark anyway, since raccoons, opossums and hungry coyotes lurked in the woods around their place. Even after the boys had turned themselves in, she kept the cat close.

Kevin lived just up the road from them. Dale had hired him and a couple of his friends two years ago to help weed and spread new gravel around the yard. Frances caught the boys sneaking a beer from the fridge they'd moved into the shed when they first cleared the garage for the store. She disliked Kevin after that, and Dale had a hard time convincing her to keep him on. "It doesn't surprise me one bit," she said when she learned of Kevin's involvement in the cat killings. "A lack of empathy for animals is one of the early signs of a sociopath. We're living next to Ted Bundy."

Dale folded the paper under his armpit, rose and joined the procession into the store, leaving the unfinished scarf on the bench. Frances already sat behind the counter, sorting the mail. She didn't look up when he entered. Chamber music poured out of the radio. Dale didn't dare comment on the selection. He pictured the way his wife would crinkle her nose if he confused Smetana's *Ma vlast* with Mozart again. Sputnik lay on her back, belly exposed, on the windowsill near the door. There hadn't been any customers yet that day, but it was still early. Dale placed the folded newspaper behind the door on a low table.

"I'm going to check the grounds, make sure nothing washed over by the woods last night." He pulled a hunter green poncho over his head. Frances murmured something and continued to sort the mail without looking up.

Dale secured the poncho's hood over his wavy salt-and-pepper hair and stepped into the rain. The gravel path that guided visitors through the labyrinth of stone faces crunched beneath his boots. He followed the slope down toward the back edge of the yard. On the perimeter, birdbaths overflowed and miniature pagodas sought shelter beneath the cropped limbs of the first barrier of Douglas firs.

The lawn accessory business hadn't been his idea. He wanted to turn the property into a tree farm, grow fruit tree saplings to sell to nurseries. But Frances didn't see the practicality in it. Trees could die. They would be at the mercy of the weather, bugs, nighttime armies of browsing deer and elk. If no one wanted the stock and it grew too large, the young trees would have to be destroyed. For Frances, statues were the smarter investment, a solid stock impervious to time.

Dale cut through the gazebo and smelled the sweet aroma of moist cedar. He paused beneath the overhang, at the center of the labyrinth, and surveyed the hazy yard. The reckless abandon and youthful exuberance displayed by the collection of pissing boys, excited by their exposure but trying to act bored, made him think of the cat killers. Frances hadn't been the only one outraged by the teens' behavior. The disgust had spread beyond those victimized, through the entire community and farther out over the airwaves and the Internet.

He remembered late one night, driving country roads his junior year with his best friend, Floyd. They'd taken their dates home and were restless. The headlights caught a pair of eyes near the ditch on the opposite side of the road. Floyd cried, *Coon, ten points!* Dale swerved the wheel and pressed the accelerator. As they approached the eyes, Dale realized the creature was too slight of build to be a raccoon. He quickly tried to right his course. But Floyd grabbed the wheel and forced him back on target. There was a thump, and Floyd crowed with triumph. Then they went on with their lives. It was a mistake, but that didn't change the loss he had caused some stranger. At times, Dale felt like he was the only one who didn't think the boys should hang.

Dale clenched his massive hands and barely heard the pop of his knuckles over the rain. As he started again toward the back, he caught a glimpse of the old garden patch behind the shed, weedy and overgrown from years of neglect. The garden had been Frances's project. She'd planted both vegetables and flowers. Most of the first crops were choked out from the shade cast by the canopy of the nearby forest, but she wanted to raise the kids on fresh food. And her persistence paid off. Year after year he watched her take pride in that strip of soil. Dale was positive that, in those days, she would have been receptive to the idea of a tree farm.

But that was before they stopped trying to have children. Four pregnancies in six years, all miscarriages, except for Jacob. Frances had carried him to full term, and she enjoyed the anticipation, the way all their friends and family fussed over her. Her coworkers at the bank had thrown her a baby shower. She'd even rescued Sputnik from a barn, with the idea that the kitten and Jacob could grow up together.

Then on a rainy night in October twelve years ago, Dale drove her to the hospital in Portland. Nearly a day later their little boy emerged. Jacob weighed exactly seven pounds. He had slate gray eyes and lots of wavy blonde hair. And he was dead. Frances made clear there wouldn't be any more. And she lost interest in her garden.

He continued past the pump house toward the back fence line. Beyond the mesh wire, the Gifford Pinchot National Forest stretched for miles. Their place was part of an old homestead that used to protrude into the forest. Dale remembered that the previous owner had warned him of an old well, lost somewhere in the underbrush. *Only a damn fool would go stomping around back there,* he said. *Fall down that well, nobody ever gonna hear from you again.* Dale had searched for the well for months before Jacob was born, worried that he would wander off and fall through. Now he didn't care; he didn't hunt or have any other reason to enter these woods.

At the fence, Dale leaned against one of the posts. He followed the paths of raccoons and possums, thin mud strips, with trajectories traced in bent leaves of grass by the fence. Their paths led under and through the wire, straight to the feeders. They would shake loose some stale or molding seeds, then creep back to the woods. He had warned Frances this would happen if they started feeding the birds. But she insisted that customers would buy more feeders if they saw them in action.

You couldn't really blame the scavengers, he thought; the seed piles provided an easy and constant meal. Without a dog, Dale knew any defense of the feeders was futile. But he wasn't allowed anything that might upset Sputnik. So, under the cover of night, the seed was stolen and the deer ate the tulips. Sputnik stayed inside at night and Frances pestered Dale about every pair of glowing eyes she found peering from the darkness.

He would run out, slapping a broom handle on the porch and shouting obscenities. The little bastards just retreated to the trees and waited for the house lights to go out before resuming their feast. Frances fussed over the way he handled the raccoons and opossums. He didn't need to use such coarse language. *It's the tone not the words,* she tried to explain, *it's not like they understand English.* But the way the bold ones stared him down, smirking at his pointless routine, Dale knew the beasts understood more than his wife gave them credit for.

Dale scanned the statues at the back of the property. Every few months Frances made him rearrange the stock, based on what some garden magazine said was popular. Customers needed easy access to the fashionable ornaments. If a statue out by the fence sold, that was a bonus. Dale noticed that one of the long-term residents of his yard was missing. The figure was the last of a shipment of female ascetics that Frances had bought in a fit of feminism. They had proven less popular than the Buddhas or the saintly Catholic women.

The stone penitent demurely wore long, simple robes that hid her womanly features. Her hair was pulled into a bun and held in place by a plain shell comb. The eyes were partially closed, as the woman's head tilted downward on her slender neck toward a water bowl she held in front of her chest with both hands. The little Asian woman was the only statue Dale enjoyed seeing in the sales yard because she didn't stare at him.

He wondered if the ascetic had finally been sold. It seemed unlikely that he wouldn't notice the sale. Dale and Frances were the only employees of the shop and moving and loading the statues was his job. Dale stared into the forest, up the steep evergreen slope choked with salal and blackberry vines, as far into the mist and shadows as his vision allowed. There were no obvious human trails through the brush. But where the bushes just began to be obscured by fog, surrounded by a thicket of sword ferns, he thought he could see a gray stone. It didn't look natural, far too smooth and erect, with a slender build. It had to be the missing statue, Dale thought. But when he whipped the droplets from his glasses and looked again, the gray image was gone.

Dale walked back to the store. Nothing had changed: no customers, the cool cement walls echoed with classical music, Sputnik remained comatose on the windowsill. Frances had finished sorting the mail and was flipping through a catalog. She looked up at the sound of the bell when the door opened. Her expression didn't hide her disappointment that it was merely Dale returning and not a customer. Dale removed his poncho and hung it in the corner.

"Did we finally sell that little Asian woman?"

Frances set the catalog down on the counter. She scrunched her forehead and looked at her husband. "Not that I'm aware of. Is she gone?"

Could she have been stolen? It seemed like an awful lot of effort to drag a lawn ornament out through the brush. And he doubted the cement figure would have much resale value. He shrugged. "I must've just missed her."

They settled into their places in the shop, and didn't speak for the rest of the day. The rain poured down steadily, through the day and into the evening. No one came by to browse the statues or stock up on birdseed. It didn't surprise Dale; business always slowed during the fall, as the weather worsened and people turned their attention inside.

After they closed and moved to the house, the sound of rain on the roof was like white noise, filling the lengthening silences that crept through the rooms when the music and television were off. Frances breathed heavily, tapping a pen on her annotated and illustrated book about birds. Dale knitted and watched the evening news. More outrage and calls for vengeance on the cat killers. He shook his head at the weather segment and the poor young reporter, forced to stand out in a parking lot for the live shot. *As you can see here, John, it's still raining,* hunched over the microphone as she pointed at a puddle, *with another two inches expected overnight.*

Frances sat near the fire reading, Sputnik in her lap. She clicked her tongue at the cat. Periodically, she asked him to turn the TV down. Then she looked out the window, and her voice grew weary. "They're back, Dale."

Dale pulled on his shoes and went to the kitchen to get the broom. He peered around the edge of the sliding glass door. A fat mama raccoon and three babies clustered beneath the largest feeder. The mama shook the feeder's pole, dumping seed on the ground below. With one hand on the outside light switch and the other grasping the door handle and broom, Dale watched as the family sifted through the mud for something to eat.

"Remember, you don't have to cuss at them to scare them off."

He switched on the light as he flung the door open. Dale sprung onto the porch, beating the broom against the boards and shouting "Merry Christmas and a Happy New Year, you dirty little bastards!" The three smaller raccoons shot off toward the forest. Mama raccoon reared up, teetering on her hind legs, her front paws swaying in the rain like a boxer. Dale chucked the broom at her, and she took off.

He could tell the raccoons were inexperienced at stealing food from humans. They had frightened easily, and fled completely out of the yard. The really fat males would simply conceal themselves nearby until the lights went out. Mama might convince the little ones to try the feeder again tonight, but they would approach with caution.

Dale retrieved the broom from the yard. Mud-covered seeds clung to his shoes. As he approached the porch, something ran past his legs and into the darkness.

"Oh Dale," Frances said from the doorway. "You didn't shut the slider behind you. Sputnik got out."

"Are you sure?" He looked around the living room but saw no sign of the cat.

"Of course I'm sure. She jumped right out of my lap when you started hollering."

"I'm sure she'll come back up."

"Not if she runs into those raccoons."

Dale sighed and began to change into his rubber boots. "I'll go look for her." He pulled on his rain slicker and grabbed a flashlight from the closet.

Outside, he remembered one of his grandfather's favorite expressions: *A chicken has a brain the size of a pea, and even it knows to get in out of the rain.* What the hell was wrong with that miserable cat? Calling for Sputnik, he trudged through the downpour. He could feel the stares from row after row of unseen stone faces, hidden in the night. His light barely penetrated the darkness, only illuminating their empty eyes when they were a few feet in front of him.

Dale reasoned that the cat must have made for cover from the relentless rain. He checked under the porch, the gazebo, beneath the fence line trees, and the eaves of the shed and pump house. No sign of Sputnik. Behind him, Frances called from the door; he could hear the fear in her increasingly distressed tone. He stood at the back fence, cursing the cat, when he heard something rustle out in the woods. "Sputnik," he called. Over the pelting sound, he could barely discern the ringing of the small collar bell.

Dale hoisted himself over the fence, using the nearest post for leverage. He tromped through the undergrowth toward the bell. Vines reached out to ensnare him, snagging his coat and wrapping around his legs as he passed. A strap from the bottom of the flashlight chafed his right wrist. He kept a grip on the flashlight, slowly moving the beam from side to side. With his free hand, he felt his way forward, groping the rough bark of the trees, pushing aside the barely visible branches. With each step the ringing grew clearer, louder.

He entered a clearing, glad to walk upright for a moment, free of the blackberry's piercing thorns. Across the clearing, he heard something moving toward him, too large to be Sputnik. Then with a crack the ground gave way beneath him. Dale barely caught himself on the remaining boards on the old well's far lip. Below, he heard the sharp thuds of rotten pieces of boards, and his flashlight, ricocheting down. There was a metallic clank as the light hit bottom, but no splash. His chin dug into the soggy ground. He tried to prop himself up on his elbows and push himself out with his legs. The walls of the well were strangely dry and brittle after the slippery mud of the forest floor. The dirt sloughed off beneath his boots; Dale's efforts only dropped him further down the side.

As he hung there, with only his hands above the surface, he realized that the ringing had stopped. His face turned toward the bottom. He could see nothing, not even his own body dangling. He breathed deeply, and the air was surprisingly sweet and fresh, not stagnant at all. It was warm, and the warmth enveloped his body with each breath. He felt the darkness fill his lungs and permeate out through his bones. He felt light. He hung there and stared into the darkness, expectant, waiting for something to happen, just like when he was a child testing the troll.

For a moment Dale considered allowing himself to drop. How easy it would be to give himself to the darkness. He wouldn't have to face the stares of the statues. The empty rooms. The memory of his son. All he had to do was let go.

Then his left hand slipped. Swinging from one arm, his side struck the wall, and jolted him back. He remembered Frances. She was waiting for him to bring Sputnik back. Waiting for him, and he wanted to go back to her.

Dale kicked his legs against the sides, desperate to find some kind of footing. The wall chipped away with each blow of his feet, until his toes rested on a narrow root. He swung his left hand further out, groping along the forest floor for something to grip. His hand grasped a smooth, narrow stone. Dale wrapped his fingers around the cold surface. The stone slid back, giving under his weight, then caught long enough for him to secure his position.

With his other hand, Dale grasped a sapling. He strained with his upper body, releasing the stone to pull with both hands. The tree bent beneath his weight. Head above the rim, he braced one arm on the ground by the well.

Dale scrambled over the edge and collapsed onto the forest floor. He rolled onto his back, cold, gulping wet air. He could not feel the stone he had first used for leverage against his back. Beyond the clearing, he could hear something move through the brush toward the house, but he couldn't make it out. His glasses were smeared with mud; he wiped the lenses and rubbed his eyes. Sputnik rubbed against his elbow, purring. He grabbed the cat and held her tightly to his chest with both arms.

As he approached the house, Sputnik butted his chin with her head. Dale flicked the little bell on her collar. Frances waited for them on the porch, hands clasped together and pressed against her face.

Frances's eyes watered as she suppressed tears. In her eyes Dale thought he caught a familiar concern. A concern not just for the cat but for him as well. A look he recognized when he returned from an errand and she thought he had been gone too long. Or when she'd heard about an accident at the mill. A look he wasn't sure he'd seen since they both held Jacob's body between them. She took Sputnik, and led Dale into the house, clutching his arm until they sat by the fireplace. "What happened out there? Where was she?"

Dale shook his head, unsure what to tell her. Unsure what to tell himself. What had retreated, just out of sight in the brush? What was the seductive feeling in the darkness of the well? "Just out in the woods."

"You look terrible."

He was a wreck, clothes snagged, torn and covered in mud. He could feel several puncture wounds throbbing on his legs. His arms felt hollow and he anticipated several bruises tomorrow. "It all looks worse than it really is. Bumped into a couple blackberries, tripped over a stump, and of course the ground is saturated. Just glad I found Sputnik." He scratched the cat under her chin. "I think I'm gonna get out of these clothes, wash up and head to bed."

Dale slipped off his boots and started for the bedroom. But he paused as he passed Frances, and kissed her on the forehead. His hand rested on her shoulder, and he felt a slight tremble. She placed her own hand on top of his, reluctant to let him pass.

In bed Dale lay and listened to the slanting rain pound the window. He felt helpless, as he replayed how easily he could have fallen. Frances lay next to him, with Sputnik curled in a ball on her chest. Dale wondered if he'd done everything he could to protect her. She breathed deep, stretched and sank deeper into her pillow.

Dale resolved to fill in the well. He'd hire Kevin to help him fill it with stones. Dale had always liked the kid and, despite Frances's feelings, thought he could use a second chance. The labor might help Kevin figure out more constructive ways of occupying his time. Satisfied with his plan, though stiff and sore, Dale finally managed to drift off to sleep.

By morning the clouds had passed, giving way to a cool fall day. After breakfast, Dale and Frances walked out to the gazebo. Steam rose off the display yard under the midmorning sun. Finches splashed in the ebbing birdbaths and there, at the corner of the shed, Dale noticed the little ascetic. He couldn't remember moving her, but told himself that he must have.

Dale and Frances leaned on the gazebo rail, and stared toward the garden. "Say Franny, why don't we turn that old garden into an orchard? We could grow apples, pears, maybe some plums or cherries." Kevin could help plant the trees. And Dale decided to keep the little ascetic. He imaged how good she would look beneath a canopy of blossoms.

"Still got it in your head to sell trees?"

"Nah," he said, "these trees would just be for us."

Minidoka Swing

Kenji Yamamoto's cigarette smoldered in an ashtray in the kitchen. He had always made a point of not smoking around his grandchildren. Outside the rain beat out a steady rhythm on the windowpane. The late spring shower washed away the last bits of winter's grime before ushering in another temperate Portland summer. Kenji's fingers and knees creaked as he crossed the room; the moisture aggravated his arthritis, causing him to wince as he shuffled about the gray living room. He wore a pair of house slippers, pants held high with suspenders and a blue and green striped sweater. His narrow face was elongated by a little white beard. Atop his head, his salt and pepper hair was thinning.

The Yamamotos' apartment was sparsely decorated. Traditional *tatami* mats, woven from soft rush straw, covered the hardwood floor. Against one wall stood an upright Yamaha piano. Family photographs were displayed across the top, along with a card from Kenji's 81st birthday. Next to the piano was a small, black-lacquered table with a record player and metronome. The metronome's arm swung in time with the rain, clicking out the same steady rhythm.

Michelle, Kenji's 17-year-old granddaughter, sat at the piano bench, mouthing her clarinet's reed and looking like a *koi* fish. Patiently, she waited for Kenji to drag his stiff body over and assemble his trumpet. Michelle knew how the weather restricted her grandfather's motion. Usually she used these times to study the old photographs.

There were pictures of Kenji and his older brother, stern faced in their army uniforms, of her mother, along with aunt and uncle as children, and two generations of weddings. The only wedding not depicted was Kenji's own. Her favorite photo was of her grandmother in a silk *kimono* embroidered with cherry blossoms, with her hair gathered in a small *mage* bun, accented by a pearl *kushi* comb. Michelle thought the most striking aspect of the picture was her grandmother's expression. The face looked sad, while the eyes burned with joy, as though her heart was breaking in the same instant she was falling in love.

Her grandfather continued to saunter over, polishing his dented trumpet on his shirt. Michelle warmed up, her fingers instinctively moving through exercises. There was no hurry; they had the apartment and the afternoon to themselves.

###

A block away, Kenji's wife, Hiroko, made little origami cranes from paper with the other church ladies. The ladies folded the birds carefully, being sure not to rip the delicate paper. The crane was a symbol of peace and long life. The mythic bird was often given to the ill, to wish them a quick recovery. This afternoon, the ladies would make over 11,000.

The cranes were for the annual pilgrimage to Idaho by former detainees of the Minidoka Relocation Center and their relatives. These cranes would be placed at the memorial to represent peace. It was believed that 1,000 cranes would make a wish come true. The Epworth Methodist Church was working with the group, Friends of Minidoka.

###

Michelle started taking music lessons from her grandfather when she was eleven years old. She had come a long way from the strangling goose sounds she produced when she first picked up the instrument. In recent years their lessons had become more ritual than educational. She was a gifted girl, first chair in the high school orchestra and a member of the jazz band. Despite her success, she kept coming every week to see the old man. Their lessons gave him a purpose and kept him out of her grandmother's way, at least for the afternoon. Michelle was willing to keep coming as long as it continued to please both her grandparents.

Their long afternoons playing old jazz, blues and swing also offered Michelle a chance to piece together her family's past. She knew that both her grandparents had been interned during the war, but no one ever talked about Minidoka. In school, the subject of internment was glossed over, more a footnote in a bland history textbook than an actual event. Direct questions about the subject were met with somber and tight-lipped replies from her family. Sometimes, she tried to trick her grandfather into giving something away, but she was rarely successful.

She turned to her grandfather as he continued to hobble across the room and asked, "Grandfather, what happened to grandmother's beautiful *kimono*?"

"Oh, it was lost during a move years ago." But Kenji knew exactly when the loss had occurred. Hiroko's *kimono* had been confiscated and inventoried by the government at her family's home in Eugene before relocation. Family heirlooms were supposed to be returned after the war, but never were. Kenji remembered his father burying tea sets in the backyard, and hiding crates of *kimonos*, fans and scrolls beneath the old porch. His father never returned to look for the items, unable to bring himself to ask the new owners for permission to enter his own home.

"Which move was it?"

"I can't recall."

Kenji knew of his granddaughter's obsession with the past, but didn't indulge it. Kenji and his family were forced to leave their possessions and home in Southeast Portland. They didn't get to choose where they lived or what they ate. While their sons and daughters served the United States abroad, the internees were robbed.

But it was over now. He saw little point in dwelling on the past. He was "American," and brooding on that subject could only cause unforgivable rifts between his family and their adopted country. His forgiveness would not come from words.

###

Their lessons were always the same. They played Kenji's favorite songs from his youth, *Careless, When the Swallows Come Back to Capistrano,* and *The Lady's in Love With You.* Occasionally, Michelle rehearsed her school songs for him, but only if she needed pointers on a piece or was nervous about a big performance. Usually those numbers were kept secret so they would be fresh to Kenji when he attended the recitals and concerts. They played duets, either clarinet and trumpet, or clarinet and piano. The songs always left Kenji feeling nostalgic for his performing days.

"How about we start with *Boogie Woogie* today?" Kenji coughed as he sat down on the bench next to Michelle. He adjusted the metronome, tapped his foot and snapped his stiff fingers to count them in. The swift and steady tempo of the song had always reminded Kenji of a train rumbling down the track. The peppy little number perked both of them up on this dreary afternoon.

After each song Kenji would adjust the metronome and call out the next number. Both knew all by heart. As they played, Kenji didn't just tap out the rhythm with his foot, he moved with the beat, his legs bouncing in and out, feet flopping around like dead fish, as though he would start dancing at any moment. Yet no matter how sporadic his motions may have seemed, they were always in time.

Normally Kenji and Michelle would play for a good two hours before calling it quits. Today was different. After five songs Kenji had to stop. The trumpet's keys and rhythmic dancing had taken their toll on his joints. Outside, he heard the rain change to a blues tempo, as if it sensed his pain.

"Are you alright, Grandfather?"

"I just can't grip the keys. Would you keep playing for me?"

Michelle nodded.

He put down his trumpet, hammered out the first few chords of the next piece on the piano, and waited for Michelle to pick up the song by ear.

She meditatively moved her fingers on the clarinet's keys, not making a sound. In her head she played the notes, checking them before revealing them for her grandfather's scrutiny. When she was at last confident that she had the melody, she began to play.

The song was one of his favorites, an old Jimmy and Tommy Dorsey number, *This Love of Mine*. Outside, the rain let up, complying with the rhythm of the song. Kenji closed his eyes and the lyrics came to him out of the mist. His mouth started moving in recognition, like Michelle's fingers, before any sound came out. Eventually, carried away by the music and the rain, he began to sing in a trembling voice:

> *This love of mine goes on and on,*
> *though life is empty since you have gone.*
> *You're always on my mind, though out of sight.*
> *It's lonesome through the day,*
> *and oh, the night!*
>
> *I cry my heart out it's bound to break,*
> *since nothing matters, let it break.*
> *I ask the sun and the moon,*
> *the stars that shine,*
> *what's to become of it, this love of mine?*

At first his voice cracked from a dry throat. The sound was bittersweet, a raspier tone than in his youth. His vocal chords had been ravished by years of smoking and neglect. He hadn't sung anything more than *Happy Birthday* in the years since he left the Minidoka Relocation Center to join the army. *This Love of Mine* had been the heart of his band's set list, and it took Kenji back to a world locked behind barbed wire, where dust got everywhere, in boots and hair, inside the tarpaper barracks, which didn't matter because it was impossible to keep the raised wood floor clean. For a moment he could almost taste the dust again. He remembered how he and his friends had organized dances in the mess hall on Saturday nights. They had formed a band, *The Norakuro Band,* and played songs by Jimmy and Tommy Dorsey, and Glenn Miller. Traditional Japanese songs were also worked into the set list throughout the evening...

###

...Everyone, young and old, turned out to dance. The youth prided themselves on their dancing, much like other American kids. The men dusted off worn suits, while the women put up their hair, and put on the brightest dresses they could find. Consumed by the sweltering sea of bodies, a person could forget that they were in a single long room, with no windows or insulation, and poor ventilation. A light dust cloud hung over the crowd, as they stomped and dragged their feet to the beat.

Kenji played piano and trumpet, and occasionally sang with the band. *The Norakura Band* was popular; they kept spirits high and made life behind "the wire" bearable. Their suits never fully matched, but came close with various blue coats and red ties. *The Norakura Band* may have been ragtag, but Kenji had felt glamorous whenever the crowd cheered. More than anything else, those big band songs helped the community feel like they were still part of the country...

###

...As the song ended, Kenji found himself looking at the pictures on the piano. His gray-blue eyes shimmered with suppressed tears as he looked from the pictures to his granddaughter's smiling face. With a shaking hand he patted her on the leg.

"Have I ever told you why there aren't any pictures of my wedding?"

Michelle shook her head excitedly. She didn't speak, fearful that he would change his mind and abandon this tangent.

"It was during the war. I was eighteen and had just been drafted. Your grandmother was your age at the time. She was pretty like you, too. But we were far from our homes here in Oregon. They had sent us out to Idaho with nothing. We got married in the camp before I left and there weren't any cameras, let alone photographers available. That *kimono* you asked about in the picture was supposed to be your grandmother's wedding *kimono,* but we didn't have that. It was hard for her to go through the ceremony without it." Kenji paused; he could see sadness creeping into Michelle's eyes. "Despite our limitations, it was a beautiful service. The mess hall never looked so appealing; all we did was put up some paper lanterns. Our friends and family were there, and the band I formed played for us. We may not have had pictures, fancy clothes, or a big cake, but we did get a first dance as man and wife."

"That sounds nice."

"It was simple, but nice."

Michelle smiled to herself. She wasn't sure if it was the song, the pictures or the rain that made her grandfather open up, but she didn't care. It was exactly the type of memory she longed to hear, a moment of normalcy despite this hardship. Michelle often wondered how it was possible to live through something as degrading as interment and come out with a positive attitude.

"Why don't we call it a day?" Kenji said, as he reached over to the record player. While he flipped the switch and dropped the needle into the vinyl grooves, he wondered if Michelle understood how much these songs meant to him. Glenn Miller's *In the Mood* crackled out of the older speaker. Kenji licked his lips in contemplation, and decided that next year they would all go to Idaho. Michelle and he would expand their repertoire and give one last performance in his old venue. They could perform for the other pilgrims. Maybe some of the old guys would even be there.

With renewed spirit, and confidence in his plan, Kenji slowly rose to his feet. Quivering at the ankles he shuffled his way around the piano bench, then stood directly before Michelle. In a slight bow he held his hand out to his granddaughter.

"May I have this dance?" he playfully inquired.

Michelle sprang from the bench and answered her grandfather's request with a little curtsy, then regally took his proffered hand.

"Now, let me show you how we used to dance. Real music deserves dancing, not all that jumping around you kids do." Kenji took both of his granddaughter's hands in his own. He stepped back on his left foot and rocked on his right. "That's it Michelle, you're doing the West Coast Swing...rock, step, triple step, triple step..."

Once they got in the groove, Kenji released her right hand and led his granddaughter through a turn. They both laughed and spun slowly across the straw mats that covered the floor. *In the Mood* ran circles around them. Instead of the quick steps urged by the horns and drums, they complied with the rhythm of Kenji's body, a little less, even, than half time, yet infectious nonetheless.

The next song was a ballad, *Moonlight Serenade,* and Michelle was relieved for her grandfather. They moved to the closed position. This tempo was more manageable, and they danced in perfect time. Still, she feared the activity would wear him out and aggravate the pain in his joints. But when she looked at him, he didn't wince; he just smiled with bright eyes. Outside the rain poured down. The thought they were dancing in the same way he and grandmother must have danced, all those years ago, to the same song, brought a smile to Michelle's face, a stolen moment together. Firmly in her grandfather's grasp, Michelle closed her eyes, trusting in his lead as she imagined her grandparents' wedding...

...Grandfather stepped down from the stage to join his wife, wearing a worn but clean navy blue suit, with gold buttons that shone like stars, and gray pinstripes. His white shirt, dyed a dull yellow by the dust, was topped by a red bowtie. Grandmother wore a matching tan linen skirt and jacket, made elegant by a beautiful beige silk blouse. Her hair looked glamorous, shiny and black with cascading tresses. As they took each other's hands to dance, the scene resembled a picture Michelle had seen of the couple post-war: Grandfather in his olive green dress uniform, Grandmother balancing Aunt Leah as a baby on her hip. Except in this picture the young newlyweds can't stop smiling. The rest of the band began to play *This Love of Mine,* as Kenji sang softly to his bride. Tenderly, he whispered the words into her ear, never leaving the closed position. They weren't doing the West Coast Swing, but the Minidoka Swing...

...Michelle opened her eyes. She smiled to herself. The dance was simple, but nice.

Acknowledgements

To anyone who read these stories, at any stage in their drafting, intentionally or by accident, thank you for paying attention: Sam Ligon, Greg Spatz, John Keeble, Kathryn Trueblood, Sarah Stamey, Carlos Martinez, Gary McKinney, Heather Cuthbertson, Sylvie Bertrand, Christopher X. Shade, Anita Levin, Phillipe Chatelain, Kolleen Carney Hoepfner, Ashley Perez, Diamond Braxton, John Christopher Nelson, Jordan Robson, Amy Ralston Seife, Madison Copeland, Regina Barnett, Cilla Chavez, Couri Johnson, Erin Michaela Sweeney, Robert Yune, Ericka Taylor, Elizabeth Moore, Monet Thomas, Michael Bell, Leyna Krow, Rosie Bartel, Melissa Huggins, Christine Holbert, Justin Lawrence-Daugherty, Cynthia Brandon-Slocum, Michael Pankratz, Rie Lee, Katrina Stubson, Tyler Evans, Aimee Cervenka, Laura Citino, Seth Marlin, Karen Maner, Casey Patrick, Jeff Corey, Stacy Hovland, Jennifer Moody, Mary Stravinski, Daniel Harvey, Aristides Jatos, Marissa Levien, and Corey Pung

Special thanks to William K. Lawrence and his team for taking a chance on my work and welcoming me to the Tribe.

The following stories were previously published:

"Minidoka Swing" in *Tribute to Orpheus 2* (Kearney Street Books), "Narrow River" in *Gold Man Review*, "The Dispatched" in *Cagibi*, "Omega" in *HASH*, "California Sunshine" in *In Parentheses*, "From This Day" in *Defunkt Magazine*, "Community Service" in *Drunk Monkeys*, "Killdeer" in *The Westchester Review*, "Redd" in *The Bookends Review*, "A Certain Kind of Luck" in *Twisted Vine Literary Arts Journal*, "Goodnight, Irene" in *Inlandia*, "Beware of Darkness" in *Pumpernickel House*, and "In Spite of All the Danger" in *Broken Tribe Review*.

THE AUTHOR

B. R. Lewis was born in Portland, OR, but raised across the river in the paper-mill town of Camas, WA. He graduated from Western Washington University and earned his MFA at Eastern Washington University's Inland Northwest Center for Writers in Spokane. Between degrees, he completed two terms of service with AmeriCorps in Sitka, AK and Vancouver, WA. He served as an editor for both *Willow Springs* and *Sundog Lit*. He currently lives in southern Oregon, where he teaches at Umpqua Community College. Visit B. R. Lewis at www.br-lewis.com.